JAMES E. CHANDLER, SR.

WHO'S IN MY HOUSE?

ONE MONDAY MORNING IN THE LIFE OF DEACON WILLIE A.P. LESTER, JR.

—— ◆ ——

WILLIE'S WORLD: BOOK II

—— ◆ ——

SHOWITT ENTERTAINMENT
DOUGLASVILLE, GA

ISBN 13: 978-0-99691-919-7

Published by Showitt Entertainment, Inc.
Douglasville, GA

Printed in the United States of America
First Edition November 2015

Cover Design by Make Your Mark Publishing Solutions
Interior Layout by A Reader's Perspective
Editing by Make Your Mark Publishing Solutions

WHO'S IN MY HOUSE?

ONE MONDAY MORNING IN THE LIFE
OF DEACON WILLIE A.P. LESTER, JR.

WILLIE'S WORLD: BOOK II

Acknowledgements

I would like to thank my gracious Heavenly Father, who anointed me to begin and complete this work. I would not be able to continue this series without You guiding my hand and stretching my mind. All praise, glory, and honor belong to You, and I lift up Your name.

In the beginning, this book was birthed as a stage play performed at my church, Marvelous Light Christian Ministries. The cast was comprised of members of the church, and it's because of their tireless labor of love and hard work that this work was first seen by many on stage before being transformed into print.

A special thank you goes to Kelly Chandler, my wife and best friend, who believed from the very beginning and never doubted I could accomplish this God-given assignment. I love you for being the most incredible woman I've ever known in my life and a virtuous woman in every way. Thank you for reading every chapter I wrote without complaining. Thank you for fixing and drinking coffee with me at all hours of the night as this book and the plays were being deposited into my spirit. Thank you for holding me up and lifting me up before the Lord. You've been my rock, and I am who I am today because of you. Get ready, my love, the best is yet to come for both of us.

Kayla, J.C., Jonathan, my children who have always given me unconditional and unceasing love and constant support, know that you are the reason why I push as hard as I do to make a difference. You inspire me more than you know, and I'm humbled and honored to have been entrusted with such gifted, intelligent, spirit-filled, and amazing children. You are my inspirations and I love you and thank you for all you've done for your mom and me. I would not dare forget to acknowledge and thank my precious grandbaby, Lauryn. You're always so concerned about PaPa and wanting to let me know that everything's going to be all right. Your smile and heart are the motivation I need to be better every day.

What can I say about my sister-in-Christ and business partner Cindy? You are a constant source of energy and strength, who always comes up with great ideas to expand the reach of my ministry. Your prayers pushed me to never give up. Thank you for being a true friend to my girl and praying for her and me daily.

Thank you Dad, Mom, David, Loretta, and Cloretta, my family, who honor me by allowing me to serve as your pastor. Our parents taught us as children to work together in ministry for the glory of God, but I never imagined that I would stand as your pastor in this season of our lives. I'm grateful to have your love and I'm always blessed by your gifts to the kingdom.

I would be remiss if I didn't give thanks to those incredible members who trusted their pastor's vision by performing in the play several years ago. I truly thank you Dwain, Princilla, Tonya, Porsha, and Stanphanie. I also must thank God for the best church family in the whole world. Marvelous Light Christian Ministries, I love each of you with all my heart and I appreciate your support and prayers.

Finally, to a special young lady, who I've yet to meet in person, but have already discovered how much of a blessing she is to this book and me. Thank you, Monique Mensah and Make Your Mark Publishing Solutions. From the first day we spoke on the phone, I knew that God directed me to the right person to edit and publish this work. You were very patient with me and I appreciate your honesty and integrity.

To all of the readers who can identify with knowing one of these characters or who have laughed at the funny things that happen sometimes in church, I hope once you've read this book you'll continue to laugh and eagerly await the third volume. Remember, if you look hard enough, you'll see God moving in every situation.

INTRODUCTION

I'VE BEEN A MEMBER OF AUBURN AVENUE BAPTIST CHURCH FOR more than thirty years, and it's been a pleasure serving as the chairman of the deacon board this past decade. Collectively, the board of deacons have done a lot of good work for the community over the years, and I'm proud to have implemented some groundbreaking projects that are still making a difference today. The Jammin' 4 Jesus Athletic Ministry is strong, and we're interviewing prospective new coaches to accommodate the rapid growth of interested youth. The Hellen G. Cole Senior Citizen Housing Project is fully staffed and equipped with state-of-the-art amenities. I'm most proud of our veterans support group that meets weekly on Tuesday evenings and continues to grow by leaps and bounds. The church is doing well, if I say so myself. That is, if we can get rid of this preacher we've got.

Yeah, I'm sure you want to know who I'm talking about, because every time I mention the church, somebody always wants to know who the pastor is. I'm going to tell you in a minute or two—that's if I feel like it. But why is it that folk always want to know the name of the preacher? He ain't the only one that be in church, and he is certainly not the most memorable part of the worship experience. I mean okay, the preacher we have can sing, and hoop, and play the organ … blah blah blah. But that's about it. He don't lead devotion. He don't collect or count the money. He don't pay the bills or cook the chicken for church anniversary. He don't do none of that, but y'all just have to know who he is.

Well, I'm not going to tell you right now because instead of knowing who he is, you need to know who I am. I am Deacon Willie A.P. Lester Jr., but everybody who knows me calls me Willie. If anything goes down or if anybody gets down in this city, I know about it. If you need anything of value or want to meet anyone important, then you want to know Deacon Willie, trust me. Some of you may already know me, and if you do, I'm sure you remember what was happening in my life. What do you mean you don't remember? How could you not remember? It was last night! Sometimes I wonder if anybody pays attention these days.

Anyway, when I woke up yesterday, I went to church as I always do on Sunday mornings. After I sang the church folk happy and took up the offering, it was time for me to dip out. I had some money on the football game downtown and needed to get to the tailgate party at the stadium before all the barbeque was gone. I got into my car and pulled out of the parking lot. It was hot outside, so I rolled down the driver side window for some air. My throat was a little dry from the hard work I'd put in, so I opened up my reserve bottle of Hennessy to satisfy my thirst. I had only drunk a liter or so, and if anybody can handle their liquor, I can. Unfortunately, our city's finest felt differently when they pulled me over, accusing me of swerving on the road.

Well, I ended up spending the majority of the evening in a cell right next to the pastor of our church. Can you believe that? Yep, I said it. He and I were in jail. I'd been there before a time or two; so it wasn't a big deal for me. The preacher, however, was sitting in there crying like a baby and facing murder charges. I thought he did it at first but apparently, this time, I was wrong. Eventually, as the night went on, we found out that he was innocent and the judge let him go, but not before the church members showed up and showed their tails in the lobby of the precinct.

Thankfully, our stay was no more than a few hours, but last night was certainly one of the craziest times in my life. A good Samaritan posted my bail and the judge finally let me go too. It was insane, no doubt, and I thought it was over. Yep, I thought it was, until I made it back home.

It's Monday night, and I'm sitting here at my kitchen table, reflecting on the events of this morning. I thought I was going to spend a quiet, peaceful time alone in my apartment, but that didn't happen. I walked into my door, pulled my hat off, and got ready to make a call on my cell phone. I was about to call one of my boys when I looked up and realized something was terribly wrong. I almost dropped the phone on the floor, and before I knew it, I was yelling at the top of my lungs ...

"Who is in my house?"

Chapter 1: Willie's HOME

"I long, as does every human being, to be at home wherever I find myself." ~Maya Angelou

LET'S BEGIN WAY BACK AT THE BEGINNING. I GREW UP VERY POOR and experienced a lot of things that contributed to my broken spirit as a child. I'm the youngest of three born to my mother, but I've always felt I was an only child. I hate that I never got a chance to know my big brother. He was thirteen when I was born, but was hit and killed by a car a month before my second birthday. My sister, Betty-Jean, is ten years older than me, but since we all have different fathers, she was regularly shuffled back and forth between her dad's house and ours. I'm embarrassed to say, but it's hard for me to remember much about my biological father, including his face or the sound of his voice. He walked out on Mom and me the summer I started kindergarten.

Growing up, the only man in my life was my mom's fourth husband, who was very strict and extremely mean. His drug of choice was heroine, and each time he reached his high, it intensified our torment. I absorbed the greatest demonstration of his abuse because I'd always jump in and try to prevent him from putting his hands on my mother. He didn't like me, and to be honest, I didn't much care for him either; so I would put up the best defense I could, even though my efforts were no match for his size and strength. The only consolation was that each day I was getting stronger, and because of his addiction, he was getting weaker.

I really didn't enjoy my life as a kid, and there were times in elementary school when I thought about checking out early forever. I probably would have, had it not been for my granny. She lived about a mile from us, and whenever things got bad at home, she'd always let me come over and stay with her. I moved into her house in the seventh grade, and things got so much better. She taught me about having faith in Jesus and that prayer would change even the worst things in my life. Granny said that if you look hard enough, you'll see God moving in every situation. I've never known anyone as devoted and dedicated to God as she was. She was my rock and when she died, it left such an empty hole in my heart. I miss her, but I'll always remember the good times we had.

I turned seventeen a few weeks after Granny's death. And for me, it was either join a gang or join the military. Most of my friends were deeply involved in underhanded activities, doing time in jail, or had been killed dealing drugs on the corner. I knew if I didn't get out, it was only a matter of time for me as well. Options were limited and time to make constructive moves was rapidly decreasing. The little boy who was thrown out of the house by an abusive stepfather was long gone, and all that remained was a young teenager, who was about to give almost twenty years of his life to Uncle Sam.

In a matter of days, I was standing before the major, being sworn in. I vowed to support and defend the United States constitution against all enemies, foreign and domestic. I took my oath very seriously and served with honor. I was a soldier's soldier and rose quickly up the ranks. I gave my country the best of me, which meant three tours overseas, fighting in some of the most dreadful terrain on the face of the earth. I saw things in Vietnam that no decent man should have to see. I loved the Core and gave it the best I could. I would have given even more, but a roadside bombing ended my active career earlier than planned.

I spent the next several months in and out of hospitals, getting cut on and bandaged up by one doctor after the other. Metal shrapnel had torn into my body, and the injuries were widespread and severe. I eventually recovered from all of my wounds, but the process was lengthy and exhausting. At times, the pain was unbearable. And when the meds no longer blocked it, the alcohol did. Until then, I only drank socially. You know, with the guys in my unit.

After twenty-three surgeries, skin graphs, rehab, and therapy, I was well enough to go home. I was *so* ready to go home, but there was a small problem ... I didn't have a home to go to. I never returned to my birth town; rather, I headed out to make a new life in the big, black mecca, Atlanta. I checked into a hotel on the south side and spent a few weeks looking for a decent place to live. I had been here several times before, but never stayed more than thirty days. I loved the city, but wasn't finding the ideal place to fit me and what I wanted. I'd thought I had a life here at one time, but now, I wasn't so sure. I was about to give up until a buddy of mine told me about a new spot that he was sure I'd like. It had recently opened and was already getting great reviews. It was located downtown, in the heart of the city, near the business district, east of Peachtree Street. I checked it out, and in a matter of days, I moved what little I had into the Madison High-Rise Apartments and Condominiums.

I was young, ambitious, cocky, and undoubtedly ready to live by my rules and make my own decisions. It was time to acclimate myself to a normal society, where there were no combative enemies trying to remove pieces of my anatomy at the orders of some politician or dictator. The first few years in my new home were nothing but exciting and fulfilling for a young stud looking to make his mark in the world. I was living the good life, the fast life, the free life. I answered to nobody but myself and God, and sometimes, not even Him. That was a long time ago.

So this morning, when the cab driver dropped me off after a ridiculous night in lockup, these were the memories dancing through my mind. Back then, I thought about all the things I wanted to do with my life, and how I was going to handle being on my own for the first time in so many years. I had always had a schedule to keep, a job to report to, or an assignment to complete. I could still hear my granny telling me to clean my room or the drill sergeant telling me to advance that hill. In a strange way, it made more sense to follow someone else's orders than to create an agenda for myself.

I opened the door of that cab, put my feet down on the morning dew, and breathed a sigh of relief that Willie was home. I tipped the driver, shook his hand, watched him drive down the road, and headed for my building. When I got inside the lobby, I went straight to the elevators, pushed the button, and waited. The doors opened and I quickly stepped inside. I was glad to be inside, and as the elevator's ascension began, the joy and relief set in. I steadily looked up at the numbers on the wall as they illuminated with each passing floor. I was a little geeked, so I started audibly counting the numbers as I drew closer to my destination. Suddenly, the motor stopped, the elevator jolted to a halt, and the doors opened. That was my cue to exit.

I stepped out, reflecting on the former glory of this building, but things had changed over the years. No longer was it a beautiful architectural achievement, built by an African American construction company; rather, it had become a haven for tenants who knew little of her past splendor. Instead of walking down the hallway on plush carpeting, my feet were met by the concrete floor, stained by dried liquor and other leftover human deposits. Instead of lightly touching the mahogany-framed African art on the walls, I was forced to step over a young lady whose vomit was still sliding out of the corners of her mouth. She lay right in the middle of the floor, begging for some change, while pushing a dirty needle into her arm and urinating on herself.

I finally made it to my door. I bent down and picked up an empty McDonald's bag that somebody had left on the floor and waved quickly at Miss Ella next door. She eyeballed me, with her nosy tail, the moment I walked up. I mean this crusty little lady watched me like I was a criminal the entire time I wrestled with this old lock. It took almost a full four minutes to jiggle and maneuver this bent key around, but it finally caught, and with a firm turn to the right, the door opened, and a brotha was home.

I was still wearing the gray pinstripe suit I had on in church yesterday and all I could think about was getting out of those rags and putting on some jeans and a t-shirt. I wasn't concerned about anything else but grabbing a beer out of the fridge and plopping my butt down on the sofa. I had missed all the games on TV yesterday, but I knew that as soon as I got ahold of my remote control, I could catch the highlights on ESPN. Hear me when I tell you, the H.N.I.C. of this castle was in his palace, and I was not trying to be bothered by anybody for anything!

My head was throbbing and I was hoping I still had some Tylenol in the bathroom cabinet. I wasn't sure if the pain was a result of all that liquor I'd had before the DUI, or if it was from having to listen to the sound of that preacher's voice in the cell next to mine most of the night. I swear he got on my last nerve with all that back and forth about his innocence and why he should have never been locked up in the first place. I figured if he would have had his pimp-daddy self in church instead of being in that hotel with that girl, he wouldn't have dealt with any of this foolishness. But anyway, I don't even want to keep talking about that. Today was a new day, and again, I was very glad to be home.

When I came inside, I thought I had walked into the wrong apartment. You see, I am serious about saving money and not blowing loot unnecessarily on frivolous things. My homeboys say that I can squeeze blood out of a nickel and if I loan you a dime, you best believe I expect all of them ten pennies to come back to me quick, fast, and in a hurry. Oh no, I don't joke about my money! So hear me when I tell you that I was pissed to the highest level of pisstivity when I walked into my door and all the freakin' lights were on!

I threw my keys on the table and tossed my coat and hat on the rack just inside the door. I could not believe that my apartment was lit up as brightly as South Las Vegas Boulevard, minus the slot machines and half-naked dancing girls. I bet that the spinning disk on my electricity meter was going around in hyper speed the way a D.J.'s turntable does at a shake-a-booty club. I stood there with my mouth wide open, wondering if I had walked out of here in a hurry and left my lights on.

I was no more than three feet into the apartment when something came over me with more force than a category five hurricane. I felt in my spirit that somebody had been here while I was gone and turned the lights on. I was looking for whoever the guilty party was. I knew there was someone, somewhere, who needed a real good cussing out. It was eight-thirty a.m. yesterday when I had left here, and there's no telling how long these lights had been on. I live alone and there is only one other person in this city who has a key to my apartment. I knew that individual was not in my place unannounced. I was mad enough to chew nails and spit rivets, no doubt, but worst of all, I didn't have anyone to blame for this but myself. I started playing back the events of yesterday morning and talking to myself as if I were a schizophrenic patient at the state hospital.

"I went to church, ended up spending the night in jail with that crazy preacher, and while I was gone, Georgia Power and these cockroaches were having a party in my house! This don't make sense at all! These bugs don't need no light, and they sure ain't gonna help me pay these bills!"

If you come into my apartment and walk down the hall, the first room you will see on your right hand side is the dining room. The lights were on in there as well, but to add insult to injury, the thermostat on the wall read eighty-six degrees! Here I was, thinking that sweat was dripping into my eyes because I was fuming about the forthcoming light bill. I thought the warmth I felt against my body was these extra thick underwear I'd recently bought on sale at Value City on the west side of town. Low and behold, the reason it felt like I was standing in the middle of the Sahara Dessert was because the heater was on maximum high.

"Father, Lord God, Jesus Christ, it's *hot* as Satan's sauna room in here! It feels like four thousand degrees in this mug! I'm about to die! Now I know I was drinking a little bit when I left outta here yesterday morning, but I didn't have *that* much to drink!"

Here I was, stomping around, screaming and cussing at the top of my lungs, feverishly trying to remember what happened. I'm normally very good about thoroughly checking my place before leaving, and I couldn't imagine that I was that careless before heading out for church. Now, it's not uncommon for me to have a little nip or two with my breakfast from time to time, but I didn't remember doing that yesterday morning.

I was banging the walls and acting a straight nut, I tell you. I was so sure that somebody was going to knock at the door and ask me to bring it down a level or two. I'm glad they didn't, however, because they would have run into that kiss-my-big-black-funky-butt spirit.

I quickly got a grip and realized I was going over the top and needed to settle down. It was time to back up a little bit and fully think about everything that had transpired. I kept telling myself to inhale and exhale calmly, until what was cloudy began to clear up. Irrational behavior in the past had put me in some predicaments from which I've spent years trying to recover; so I couldn't allow myself to walk back into another hasty move without having all of the facts. So again, I started talking to myself and doing everything in my power to resolve the state of confusion in my mind. As I said, my head was throbbing somewhat, so I may have thought one thing and actually done another.

"I wasn't drunk! I mean I wasn't *that* drunk! I mean, I don't *think* I was. Humph, was I? Oh well, I'm glad I went to the package store Saturday and bought that six pack of Bud Light, 'cause I got to have something for my throat and something to calm my nerves!"

Okay, don't judge me. Some people calm their nerves by taking a pill or sipping hot tea, but that's not my remedy. I concentrate better when I have a little wet water working its way down my throat and settling comfortably in my belly. Maybe the aroma of a freshly opened beer can comes in and removes the film of puzzlement from one's mind. I don't know, but that was my rationale and I decided to stick with it.

Right here is where somebody is really going to have to pray for me. Sitting here thinking about what happened next still causes the nerves around my spine to tighten. This was the point where the spit hit the fan. I continued walking through my place and noticed that not only were all the lights on, and not only was it Shadrach, Meshach, and Abednego's fiery furnace up in here, but there were also a bunch of clothes and trash sprawled all over my furniture. I may not have become so angry had I not seen a pair of my new K-mart special underwear hanging over the lampshade, getting torched by the lightbulb!

A glass, bottle, or jug of something alcoholic was in order now more than ever. My headache had shot up to a full-grown migraine, and before I could start trying to figure out what storm had blown into my place, I needed a swift drink. I needed to fellowship right then and there with Jack Daniels, Jim Beam, Johnny Walker, or Doctor Hennessy! It didn't matter to me which one of them was going to keep me company, but I knew that I needed to get into my refrigerator right then. I moved one of the kitchen chairs out of my way, walked over to my Kenmore, opened the door, and almost passed out. There wasn't a frickin' thing in my fridge!

"Oh, absolutely not! Oh, I know I'm about to whoop somebody's tail today! It's bad enough my beer's gone, but what son of a biscuit done drunk up all my liquor? Oh, I'm killing somebody today! I'm about to blow somebody's head slap off their shoulders!"

I was snapping and freaking out to the utmost! I was at the point of no return and started hollering for the very police that had locked my butt up yesterday. You know I didn't care at all who heard me now. I had been robbed and somebody needed to pay for what they'd done to me. Who would burst into an old man's apartment and steal his most prized possessions? I mean you've got to be some kind of low-down joker to take a man's bottles and drink them for yourself. One of these rug rats in this high-rise had snuck into my place. I knew it! I was about to go bang on every door in this building until the culprit reveled himself and gave back my liquor!

I picked up my keys and put them inside my pocket. I snatched my coat back down off the rack, and I was about to grab my hat and head out the door, when I heard my name from across the room.

Chapter 2: Willie's HOUSE GUEST

"No, truly, 'tis more than manners will; And I have heard it said, unbidden guests are often welcomest when they are gone." ~William Shakespeare

"WILLIE, WHY ARE YOU YELLIN'?" WAS ALL I HEARD, AND AS SOON as the sound of somebody's voice struck my ear, I answered the only way I knew how. I'm not a scary guy, but when you know you're supposed to be alone in your house, it makes you crazy when you discover that's not the case. For several minutes I had been in here talking to myself, expecting to only hear my baritone, so you can imagine to what degree I was trippin' when there was a raspy alto calling out my name. The voice shook me; I'm not going to lie. It scared me so badly that before I knew it, I had flipped around and dropped to the floor. I reached into my back pocket, grabbed my gun, and was about to shoot toward the voice, when I heard it again.

"Willie, didn't you hear me?" the voice said. "Why are you yelling?"

I didn't believe it! There she was, strutting out of my bedroom door in a terrycloth white robe, with a towel on her head and a piece of bologna in her mouth. She was chewing to her heart's content, as if she were the owner and operator of the Backyard's Beef, Biscuits, and Buttermilk Emporium. She appeared out of the shadows, boasting aggravated arrogance, like I had interrupted her or something. She was always doing the most. But this time she had taken the art of wretchedness to a new level. My sister Betty-Jean was here.

"Betty-Jean, what are you doing in my house? I didn't even know they let you out!" I stood there waiting for a response, but none came quickly because she was too busy tilting her head back, yawning, and scratching an itch that had apparently formed along the top portion of her right butt cheek. Apparently, it was quite important to her that the piece of meat dangling from her bottom lip would not fall as she opened her big mouth. She balanced that Oscar Mayer with the precision of a circus tightrope performer. She did that while hoisting up the bathrobe in order to get an uninhibited connection with the irritation that was bothering her down below the border. It felt as if time had stopped as I stood there, motionless, waiting on Miss Thang to stop scratching her damn self.

Finally done and realizing what I had asked, she wiped some crust out of her eyes and reluctantly joined me in the conversation. "Fool, what are you talking about? Let me out of where?"

"Betty, the last time I talked to you, you said they were working you over real hard down there at that scary farm."

"Little brother, you are so slow. I told you I just got a new job working down at the dairy farm!"

At this point, I'd lifted myself from the ground and begun slowly walking toward her. I was used to being insulted by my sister, and honestly I didn't care that much about what she'd said. What I was concerned with, however, was when and how she managed to get into my apartment. How did my sister, whom I hadn't seen in quite a while, get into my place without leaving so much as a shred of evidence for how she'd gotten in?

"Betty, how did you get in here?" I asked.

"I opened the door."

"Opened the door?"

"Yeah. It wasn't locked. How do you leave here and not lock your door?"

"Are you sure it wasn't locked?"

"Isn't that what I just said? How else would I get in here? I don't have a key!"

"Well, maybe I was a little drunk, then."

"Was drunk? Willie, you're always drunk. I don't know how anybody let you be a deacon at their church."

"Girl, I know you're not talking about how I go to church, when you haven't seen the inside of a sanctuary since the last time they raffled off an 8-track cassette deck."

"That's right, and it was rigged too! Ain't no way the pastor's wife supposed to win. Shoot, if I was sleeping with the man, I might have won too."

To comprehend the look I shot her at that moment means to understand something about her past escapades with those of the opposite sex. It would be improper and certainly un-Christlike to describe her as whorish; rather, let's refer to her as more of a welcome wagon for men in need of sexual companionship. She did not discriminate by any means, but graciously received brethren of all ethnicities, cultures, and nationalities. If I were to use a portion of a Baptist hymn to describe her motto, it would be, "If I can help somebody as a pass along, then my living would not be in vain." The help she was willing to offer, however, would make even the protective angels turn their heads and refuse to watch over her through the night.

"Well, I wasn't sleeping with him at the time," she said to acknowledge the obvious silence in the room. "I'm just saying."

I refused to be pulled into a discussion about the man or men in her life. I needed more information about her presence in my house and walking out of my bedroom without getting an invitation from me. As we continued to talk, we sat in the living room so I could resume my line of interrogation. I knew that a few years back, in an attempt to settle down, Betty had remarried.

"Betty, where's your husband? Why you not out somewhere irritating the fool out of him instead of me?"

"Oh shoot, I had enough of him, child. He had to go."

"He left you too, huh? What was that . . . husband number seven?"

"No! I haven't been married no seven times, boy. This is only number four. Besides, you can't say that about Charles. He didn't leave me."

"Oh yeah. Charlie. He was husband number three, right? Yeah, I liked old boy. He was good people. He died though, didn't he?"

"Whatever. These men don't know when they got something special. Most of them can't handle all of this good, sexy chocolate, baby."

One of the benefits of spending the night in jail is that the guards don't hardly feed you, especially on the weekend. So for the first time in my life, I appreciated that I had not eaten a thing in nearly twenty-four hours. Why? Well, when my sister chose to enlighten me about the inability of these men to handle all of her sexy chocolate, she didn't simply leave it to the imagination. She felt it necessary to offer a visual exposition. This big thing plopped her tail down in my chair, slid all the way up to the front, snatched open her robe, and exposed her right leg. Thick ash coated her skin, from her toes all the way to the thong line at the top of her thigh.

This country girl swears before God that she is as fine as the morning sun. She is the only senior citizen woman I know who still goes outside wearing hot pants and go-go boots as soon as the temperature gets above fifty degrees.

"Betty, you still the same as always, like when we were growing up as kids. You always telling a bunch o' lies. Ain't nobody thinking about your chocolate nothin'!"

"Willie, you know good and well all of your little knuckle-head friends were always trying to get with your big sister. I kept swatting them away like flies. I kept tellin' them to get on, now. Go on away from here, now!"

Turning my head and rolling my eyes were all I could do at this point because I truly didn't want to entertain any more of what my sister had to say on the subject of her delusional beauty. There was one thing for sure that everyone knew about Betty: She had no battle whatsoever with low self-esteem. There was no need to continue on this topic, however. We were about to delve into a very important subject that needed to be cleared up right away: the cluttered mess that was sprawled out all over my apartment.

"Girl, would you look at all this stuff you've got laying around here! I know I didn't have it looking like this when I left."

She looked around, unmoved and unbothered by the condition of my place. It was quite evident by her response, or lack thereof, that this was not a concern of hers in the least. She shifted in her chair to the left and then to the right, barely surveying the area. She pulled a fingernail file out of the left pocket of the bathrobe and proceeded to manicure her pinky, which was now slightly elevated. Raising one eyebrow and clearing her voice, she said something that left me baffled.

"Little brother, you need to get a cleaning service over here. Oh yeah, and do something about these little critters running around all through this place too! I could hardly sleep good in your bed last night, worrying if something was gonna crawl up in there with me."

I gasped so hard that I almost choked and drowned myself with my own saliva. This chick right here had the unmitigated gall to complain about the filth that lay before us, without even acknowledging that she was the culprit. The empty cans on the coffee table—she put them there. The cracker crumbs on my couch cushion—she put them there. The candy bar wrappings and melted chocolate on the floor—she put them there. I was trying my best to focus on one thing at a time, but the visual of her lying in my bed was overtaking me. I felt a knot forming on the right side of my neck as I thought about what or *who* she was doing on top of my Sealy Posturepedic.

"My bed? I know you did not have your rusty, dusty, nasty, stanky tail up in my bed last night!"

"Boy, I was tired when I got here! Where you think I'm gonna sleep, on this old, hard, raggedy couch?"

"No! I expect you to be at your house, in your bed!"

"By the way, you need to really do something about that mattress too. My back was tense when I got up this morning. You can't have your guests sleeping on an old mattress, with the springs coming up out of it and stuff."

By this time, I had sat down in my chair and all I could do was lean back, uncross my legs, and shake my head in utter astonishment. You think I would have been surprised, but truthfully, I wasn't. My sister has been this way since we were kids. We had shared a room and slept on bunk beds. Mom had assigned me the lower bunk, but more times than I can remember, Betty would push me out and tell me to sleep up top.

So I sat there, looking as she stood up. She began rubbing the lower sides of her back while complaining about the discomfort of my bed. She then turned around and motioned for me to massage her shoulders and work the stiffness out of her neck, as if I were her personal masseur. I looked at her like she'd lost her mind. I was waiting for the blood to stop boiling in my chest before I hauled off and said something I could not take back. As hot as I was about this, there was still one more thing I had to address and resolve, or I was going to blow a gasket. So I decided to table the discussion about my bedroom furniture. We needed to deal with something else.

"You know what, Betty? I don't want to talk to you anymore about my bed; however, what we *gonna* talk about is what happened to my juice!"

As quickly as she'd started shifting back and forth and rubbing her backside, she stopped. Without even turning around to face me and address the question on the floor, she shrugged and said, "What juice?"

That's when I lost it! I jumped straight up out of the chair, moving so fast that I accidentally banged my knee on the coffee table. It hurt like a mother and the cuss words that started flowing out of my mouth were a result of both her response and my throbbing pain. I hadn't broken the skin, but I knew a knot was forming, and this gave me another reason to go ham this early on a Monday morning.

She looked at me and walked toward the kitchen. I clutched my knee and limped along, following her while trying to keep from biting a hole in my lower lip.

"What juice? You mean you're gonna act like you don't know what I'm talking about, Betty-Jean?"

We got to the kitchen, where she pulled a chair out from underneath the table and sat down. She continued to clip and file her nails while rolling her eyes as if she was irritated by these unwarranted questions. I didn't take a seat beside her; rather, I walked straight to the refrigerator. Before opening it again, I noticed that a new box of saltines, of which I remember putting atop the fridge, had been moved and tampered with. I guess that was just one more thing to add to my list. I opened the door, and before I got a chance to deal with what I saw, she parted her lips again.

"You mean dem couple of sips you had in the fridge?"

"Couple of sips? Girl, I had half a six-pack of Bud and a bottle of Patrón in here, and it's gone!"

"Well, I was thirsty, and that's all you had! You need to get some eats up in here! And don't be yellin' at me. I ain't none of yo' child!"

"Huh?" was all I could mutter as I stood there in bewilderment.

"Some salami and cheese would be nice. Oh yeah, and some grapes too. I like grapes. You like grapes? You also need to get some fresh crackers in here, 'cause dem saltines you got up there are stale."

My mouth was wide open in shock. You could have easily driven an 18-wheeler in there. I knew my sister was pushy and most of the time cared for nobody but herself, but I didn't expect her to be so condescending, knowing good and well that she was in the wrong. I mean, who sits there, defending actions that they know are out of order and indisputable.

Perspiration flowed down the side of my face because it was still as hot as Lucifer's penthouse up in here. Bending down and sticking my head into the refrigerator helped a little bit with the outer temperature, but the heat inside of me was still churning. I moved what few items she'd left inside around, trying to find some reason not to totally blow a fuse. After confirming that there was not much left, I shut the door and proceeded to check the contents of my pantry. Yep, you already know, it too was almost completely bare. I shut the door and went back to arguing with my sister.

"Betty, you mean you gonna drink up all my drink, eat up all my food, and then complain that my saltines are stale?"

"Little brother, when was the last time you went shoppin'? You ain't hardly got nothing in here to eat. I couldn't even make me a bacon and egg sandwich this morning!"

"That's because this ain't Waffle House; this is Willie's house! Now, why don't you get your clothes back on and get up outta my—"

Things had transpired so quickly that I hadn't really taken the time to examine her attire in considerable detail. I knew that she was wearing a robe and slippers, but it didn't hit me till that second that she was wearing *my* robe and *my* slippers!

"Wait a minute! Betty-Jean, are you wearing my robe?"

Without flinching or showing any concern for my frustration, she quickly stood up and twirled around as if she were auditioning for a modeling gig. "Looks good on me, doesn't it?"

"What are you doing in my robe? You know your tail is too big to be in my ... Hey, are those my brand new slippers on your feet?"

"Well, what do you expect me to put on my feet when I get out the shower, my heels?"

"Oh, Father God, no! Your old behind sho' don't need to be wearing no high heels. That's a sight nobody wants to see."

"Old? Child, when I put on my Michael Kors six-inch black Italian leather stilettos, everybody's son be checkin' out these smokin' hot, to-die-for calf muscles right here!"

"Now, that's truly nasty on a whole other scale."

"Don't hate. Your big sister has been fine all her days!"

By now, I'm sure you can tell that it's next to impossible to win an argument with somebody who feels no shame about anything she says or does. This is the same girl who, as a teenager in school, would routinely and loudly pass gas in class and unashamedly ask others why they had a problem with the sound or aroma of her release. This was that girl who would get on a crowded subway train and start dancing in the aisle and singing at the top of her lungs whenever the mood struck her. This is that fool who while sitting in church, listening to the preacher, would take out a bag of skins from her pocketbook, and loudly chew them without regard for anyone who could hear the crunching and slurping sounds she made. The bottom line: She didn't care and I didn't either. I couldn't hold it anymore; so we started going in on one another.

"Betty, I haven't been gone twenty-four hours, and in that time you done broke into my apartment—"

"The door was unlocked."

"You've run up my electricity bill—"

"The lights were on when I got here."

"You've eaten up all my food—"

"Little brother, you didn't have that much."

"Done drunk up all my liquor—"

"I told you I was thirsty, fool!"

"Wasted all my hot water—"

"Now, I didn't do that."

"Probably done left my tub filthy dirty—"

"I told you, you need a better cleaning service."

"Put your crusty, dusty booty in my robe—"

"Wait a minute, now; I put lotion on that."

"You got yo' big, ashy feet in my new slippers—"

"My feet were cold, Willie."

"Got burn marks on my ironing board—"

"Now, I didn't know it would get so hot that fast."

"And, Betty, what in the world is that strong, musty smell?"

That's when she lifted her arms and started sniffing her armpits. To me, it appeared that she was wondering if she'd missed a critical area while bathing earlier. By the look on her face, she did not have a clue about what I was talking about. Apparently, she was accustomed to the funk. And you know we get like that sometimes, when others can smell what we can't. You couldn't miss it, though, because it was strong. It wasn't a foreign smell, and I wondered why I hadn't really picked up on it until now. I started moving closer to her, and as I did, the hint of medicinal menthol became quite clear. It was liniment.

So I lit into her and told her that we were going to have a long come-to-Jesus meeting about her disrespecting my home and my stuff. I was about to get into the grilling session when she cut me off.

"Speaking of twenty-four hours, little bruh. Where you been all night?"

Wow, it hit me like a freight train that Betty had no idea what my day had been like yesterday. I had opened Pandora's box, and if I kept talking and giving her information about my whereabouts, I'd never hear the end of it. This would be the ammunition she needed to flip the topic of our discussion and find something else to use against me. She'd put my business in the street before, and I didn't want to deal with that at all. It was time to change the subject.

"The last twenty-four hours?"

"Yes, Willie. You said you've been gone for twenty-four hours. I wanna know where you been."

"I don't want to talk about it."

"Oh no, brother deacon. You said you wanted to talk. So let's talk!"

"Never mind. We don't need to do anymore talking."

"Uh uh. No, sir. Don't just cut me off like that! I ask you about where you spent last night, and you ain't got nuthin' to say? You in here drilling me like I'm your child, but when I ask you this one question, you don't wanna talk anymore?"

I was cornered and really pinned, that is until the doorbell rang. Yes! Saved by the bell. "Who is it?" I hollered.

Chapter 3: Willie's NEIGHBOR

"The Bible tells us to love our neighbors, and also to love our enemies; probably because generally they are the same people." ~G.K. Chesterton

"WHO IS IT? I KNOW YOU DIDN'T REALLY ASK THAT STUPID QUESTION. You know durn well who it is! Don't act like you've got amnesia, fool! It's the one who's trying to sleep upstairs, but can't because of all the noise coming from down here!"

"Lord, have mercy, Jesus," was all I kept saying over and over again when I recognized the voice outside my door. I don't even want to tell you who it was banging like the police, and I sure didn't want to let her inside. Sometimes, you know that your day's about to go from bad to worse, and this was one of those times. I was already aggravated by my sister, who was raising my blood pressure, working my nerves, and smelling up my apartment with that Vicks Mentholatum ointment, and now, one of my neighbors was talking to me like I owed her some money or something.

I knew I had to say something, but I'm telling you, I was not feeling up to explaining to anyone what was going on in my place. I realize that when you live in a high-rise, you should be mindful of those who stay above and beneath you. When I'm frying catfish or cleaning chitlins, I make sure to turn on the fan and open a window to allow the aroma to escape. I've got some home training. My granny raised me right and gave me good instruction on how to be respectful of others, but I'll be dog footin' if I am supposed to take lip and demands from somebody who ain't helping me pay these bills.

I sat there at the kitchen table, tapping my foot on the floor and rubbing my temples, which were swelling with each passing second. I picked my head up from the palms of my hands and looked over there at my sister, who was sitting like a statue, staring at me and waiting for an answer regarding my whereabouts last night. I was already fooling with that, and now one of the other occupants of this building thought that I was somehow obligated to respond to her manner-less request. I had barely gotten out of jail last night, where I had to deal with two men who had gotten under my skin, and just a few hours later, I found myself confronting not one, but two women who were about to shift it to another level.

"Tina," I finally said, "I'm sorry, but everything's fine. You can go on back upstairs now and do something or somebody, whoever it is you be doing."

What did I say that for? I knew when those last words fell out of my mouth that I was in trouble. I guess the lack of sleep and food had an effect on my ability to season my words with grace. I felt some cramping in my stomach, like I needed to pass gas or something, but when I leaned over a bit and pushed, only a little pocket of air squeaked out. My equilibrium was off and I acknowledge that my quick wit was moving a tad slower than normal. Oh yeah, I forgot something else; it may have also been attributed to the couple of swigs of Everclear the cabby had let me have on the way home this morning. I'm sure that didn't help either.

Anyway, Tina didn't like what I'd said, and trust me, she let me know it in no uncertain terms.

"Upstairs? What the hell you mean go back upstairs? I'm up now; so ain't no need to go back upstairs. You must have forgot who the hell it was you were speaking to, but I'm gonna help you remember! I need to talk to your black tail, anyway, about several things going on around here. I was gonna wait till tomorrow or later on in the week, but since you're in there yelling and acting a damn fool, we might as well add that to the stuff we got to deal with! Now, dammit, open this door!"

As you can plainly see, Tina Turner Johnson is as hood as they come. She was born ghetto, and trust me when I tell you, she's gonna die ghetto. She's got a beautiful, shapely body, but the mouth of a sailor. I did my best to soften the actual words she'd used when trying to convince me to open the door, because her choice of verbiage was a little to risqué to repeat. Don't get me wrong, she's good people, without a doubt, somebody you would want on your side in a battle. She's honest and has no problem speaking her mind. The deal is, however, that she never learned the art of tactfulness. So when she gets heated, you best believe that whatever's coming up is most definitely coming out.

Tina and her family have been here longer than this building's been standing. I know that doesn't make sense, but give me a minute to explain. Remember, I told you that I moved in here a few weeks after it was built, but what I didn't tell you is that there was an old high-rise on this property before. Tina was born and raised in that building, and her family was one of the last hold-outs who had convinced the landlord to guarantee that they got one of the apartments in the new construction. This was during the time when the city poured millions into an effort to revitalize some of the inner city's dilapidated neighborhoods. So when I arrived, Tina, her sister, an older brother, and her mother were already living above me, where she still resides today.

Back then, she was only a teenager, growing up around adults who spent more time hustling in the pool halls downtown than making a living at respectable nine-to-five offices uptown. Her mentors were skilled scammers and slick talkers, who paid the rent by playing dice or selling dime bags. So-called respectable white businessmen also came through to get their recreational drug of choice. She had learned the game and learned it well, but there was also a push for her to be better than the negative influences around her. Her mother did the best she could, but she struggled with a drug addiction. They would attend church every now and then, but really only on special days like Christmas, Easter, and, of course, Mother's Day.

The years rolled on and so much around here had changed, but not Tina. Her mother passed away a few years after Tina had her baby girl, and her brother went missing a few years after I moved in. She's pretty much been the same chick she's always been. Now, however, she has two children of her own who live upstairs with her. Her son, who is actually the nephew she raised, is spending his days and nights in prison, and her daughter, Kalitha, who recently celebrated her twenty-first birthday, is literally as brassy and sassy as her mother. The one big change that's taken place, however, is that Tina is now the building manager and she has no problem reminding everyone of her position and her power.

"Willie," she continued, "don't make me go back upstairs and get my master key and open your frickin' door myself! I don't have time to play these games."

Lord knows I didn't want to deal with her this morning and although, till that point, I had been unsuccessful in getting her to leave, I thought I'd try again. I mean, what could it hurt?

"Tina, like I said, everything's fine, okay? You can go on back upstairs and lay down. I'm sure you're tired and I'm very, very sorry for the ruckus. I promise to keep it down, and I will make sure that you're not disturbed in any way."

I was speaking in a softer tone, trying to defuse the obvious tension in the air, but the other person in my apartment was not on the same page. Yep, you know it; Betty-Jean decided to open her mouth and get into a situation that had nothing to do with her.

"Willie, don't be a punk. Open the door and see who that is."

"Betty, will you be quiet? I know who it is."

"Well, who is it, fool?"

"It's just my neighbor. Now, if you be quiet and mind your business, she may go away."

Too late. I should have known that Tina was not simply standing outside in the hallway at an appropriate distance from the door. I found out later that she had her ear pressed firmly against it, listening to every word we said. I'm sure it wasn't that hard though, because Betty's never been a whisperer. I don't even think she knows the meaning or concept of talking in her soft and quiet inner voice. She's always been loud. Even at pep rallies and football games, she was the one who could be heard yelling above the cheers of the opposing fans, the marching band, and even the game announcer, who was speaking into a microphone. So Tina clearly knew that somebody else was in my apartment.

"Willie," Tina yelled, "don't make me knock this door down! I don't know what y'all doing in there, but you know I don't have no foolishness in my building! I had a late night, which you already know, and I was rudely awakened from my beauty rest. So stop clowning and let me in!"

I was about to respond, when my mother's child chimed in again, but this time what she said was somewhat muffled due to the new piece of bologna hanging out of the side of her mouth.

"She's pushy, whoever she is. I think you need to open the door and let me get a look at this hoochie on the other side."

"Betty, she's nosy, that's all. She lives upstairs and she's the building manager. Now, I don't know why you think I want her in here when I already have one uninvited house guest."

"Little bro, you may not want her in here, but it sure doesn't sound like she's planning on staying out there."

I was standing there, going back and forth with Betty-Jean, trying my best to get her to shut up so I could deal with this issue, and before I knew it, she went there. Nope, not Betty, I'm talking about Tina.

"Willie!" she hollered. "You know it's my job to check on each resident when there's a sign of trouble anywhere in this building and, joker, I can smell trouble in there!"

"That ain't trouble you smell," I said while looking annoyingly at Betty. "It's Bengay!"

Betty-Jean pushed me to the side and began walking toward the entrance. "Shut up, fool, and move out the way and let me open this door!"

I knew there was nothing more I could do or say to prevent the inevitable. In a few seconds, Tina was going to be coming in and I absolutely needed to prepare myself for the impending drama. My sister unlocked the deadbolt and slid the chain out of its secured position, and no sooner had she turned the knob than Tina pushed her way right on in.

She was no more than two feet inside when she looked at both of us like she'd seen our pictures hanging on the wall at the post office on the FBI most wanted list. She was wearing a hot pink sweater, a short black and pink skirt, fluffy animal-shaped green house shoes, and designer fishnet pantyhose. I remember thinking to myself, *Who in the world would be lying down, taking a so-called nap in that getup?*

She eyeballed the both of us back and forth and sucked her teeth. Then she rolled her eyes as if to suggest that our presence was disturbing her peace. But what put the icing on the cake is that she was standing inside my corridor, talking on her cell phone to one of her bigheaded girlfriends.

"Umph," she mumbled. "Yeah, LaQuay, he finally opened the door. Oh, he's crazy all right, but he must not know who the author and finisher of crazy is. Child, I *invented* crazy and he tried to push me to my breaking point! Huh? Yeah, girl, I'm in here now. I'm gonna check everything out and let you know later if I need to evict his old behind or not. All right ... bye."

I watched in bewilderment as she pushed the end button on her phone and tucked it back into its apparent holding place between her breasts. Without saying a word, she walked on past Betty and me and proceeded toward the living room, where she sat down in my favorite chair. The two of us stood there as if we were on the transporter platform of the USS Enterprise, waiting on Scotty or Mr. Spock to beam us back to somewhere. Anywhere would have been better than here, because with each passing moment she sat there with her legs crossed, smacking on that gum, my sister's heat level continued to rise.

Puncturing the silence, Tina said, "Mr. Willie, I'm normally a very nice and patient person, but I'm feeling a certain type of way. I hope it's just me assuming something or another, but are you tryin' to push my buttons, sir? Now, because *you* had a bad time in that tore up place last night, don't think that you can bring that madness and foolishness back over here this morning."

Part of me was hoping that her presence would cause Betty to forget about the questions she was asking me when Tina had first knocked on the door, but her comments only added fuel to the fire. Betty seemed quite perturbed by the way Tina's tail had burst inside, and she might have been ready to read her a new one until the topic of last night came back up. I guess there was no getting around telling my sister that I was locked up in jail last night and my arrival this morning was only because I'd been released a little while ago.

So Betty, too, walked into the living room and as she arrived behind the other chair, she looked back at me and asked, "Last night? Willie, what tore up place is she talking about? Where were you all night? The two of you were together?"

"Betty," I said, cutting in as quickly as I could, "will you please be quiet?"

Tina sat straight up in her chair and looked at me with a devilish smirk. "Ooooh, Willie, I see you're entertaining a little lady friend, huh? Is this an escort you picked up off the street and brought home for a quickie?"

The expression on Betty's face changed immediately, and it's hard for me to describe it other than to say she was highly ticked off by Tina's nauseating suggestion. You know it's one thing for people to say that you look like your brother, or when you talk, you sound like your brother, but for someone to insinuate that you are doing your brother … That's what you call downright nasty. It leaves a bad taste in your mouth and makes your stomach ache like you've been eating a bad bean or you've bitten into a half-cooked piece of cow tongue. It's a thought most people don't want to have, unless you live in some backwoods, country, hick town, where that sort of thing is not out of the norm. Ooh yuck! That's so gross.

Something told me that my sister was about to say something smart, and knowing her like I do, it was going to set in motion an all-out project brawl between these two women. I watched as the skin on her forehead folded. Her veins simultaneously began to protrude from each side of her neck. She bit down on her bottom lip so hard that I thought she was going to start bleeding. I imagine she was thinking hard about how to come back in a way that clearly expressed the displeasure she felt from Tina's statement. The gloves were off now and the bell had rung. All I could do was step out of the way and try not to get hit by flying insults.

Betty took one long, examining look at Tina and then turned to me and said, "Willie ... what is *this?*"

"What is this?" Tina quickly repeated. "Harriet Tubman, since I don't know you, I'm gonna act like I didn't hear that."

"Uh huh," Betty grunted.

"Allow me to introduce myself. I run this building and this neighborhood. I am the manager and queen of the Madison High-Rise Luxury Apartments and Condominiums. I run this place, sweetheart."

This was a good place to jump in and try to head off a collision, and that's exactly what I attempted to do. "OK, Tina, you've seen whatever you needed to see; so you can go on back home now. Thank you for your concern, but as you can see, we're all right and everything's fine. I'll keep the volume down. Thank you. Come on, let me walk you to the door."

Betty's hearing ain't never been the best, and this morning she confused an important part of the dialog in her attempt to make out what Tina had said. "Wait a minute," my sibling asked. "Did you say that you run condoms? What you mean? You pass out birth control, and sex toys, and stuff around here?"

You could have bought me for a nickel, and I would've turned around and given you four cents back. I could not believe my sister had literally said what she had; so I had to jump right in and clear up all of the confusion. "Betty-Jean, girl, she said *condominiums!* Where's your hearing aid? What's wrong with you? Did you forget to charge your batteries?"

Apparently, this fool Tina still thought the two of us were

more than brother and sister. She decided that she was going to take this conversation in a direction it absolutely did not need to go. "Well," she went on, "if you and the good deacon here need some, I'm sure I can help you with that. Honey, give me a minute to make a phone call and—"

"Hey!" I yelled. "This is my sister!"

"Your sister?"

"Yes, my sister!"

"Deac, I thought they stopped doing that stuff between brothers and sisters back in the Old Testament. I didn't know you was like that."

"Tina, get your mind out the gutter! What do you want?"

"Well, what you expect me to think? I mean, she's standing there in your bathrobe and everything, and I thought—"

"Yeah, I know what you thought! How about you stop thinking!"

"Whatever. I should have known better. I mean, a woman this *old* wouldn't be—"

"*Old?*" my sister quickly rebutted.

With that jab at my sister's age, it was clear that Tina was not going to let Betty's depiction of her as a "this" go unchallenged. Both of these women had grown up in tough times and developed hard exteriors. Neither would ever allow anyone to belittle her in word or deed, and they lived by the laws of the street, where decency and decorum were not often employed. Betty may have been much older than Tina, but that did not mean that she was weaker or intimidated in the least. So she began moving slowly and methodically toward Tina, pointing her finger and raising her voice.

"Old?" Betty went on. "Skeezer, have you ever been slapped into the middle of next week by an old lady?"

"Excuse me?" Tina replied, now standing in a defensive posture.

"Chick, you might be the manager of the Madison High-Rise Luxury Apartments and Condominiums, but don't let your mouth write a check your fat butt can't cash! Now, call me old again and I'll snatch all four of those remaining rotted teeth out of your mouth!"

"Lady, whoever you are, trust me when I tell you that you don't want none of this! You better check your little feisty self and sit your crusty self down before I do it for you."

Betty looked directly into Tina's eyes and was not backing down at all. She then started speaking to me, but she never removed her gaze from her target in the pink sweater.

"Willie, you said this is what y'all hired to be in charge of this building? So what, Beavis and Butthead run security detail around here? I mean it's obvious y'all can't get decent help, so you got stuck with putting *trash* like this on payroll, huh?"

I tried my best to squash the foolishness that was going on between the two of them, but their engines were already on and the pedal was to the floor. I couldn't get a word in and, honestly, I was too tired to keep trying.

"Oh, no you didn't!" Tina shouted. "Moms Mabely, you don't know me. You don't want none of this right here!"

"You right about that!" Betty shot back. "Because they don't have a cure for what you got right here!"

"It's too early in the morning for this. Willie, you better put a leash on your pet before I stick a muzzle on her mouth."

"Oh hell to the no! What did you call me? I'm a dog? Somebody's pet?"

"Like I said earlier, I came down here to do my Christian duty, which was to find out what all the pandemonium was about. I had no idea that I was going to run into Kunta Kinte's grandmama instead."

51

"You see, Willie ..." Betty paused. "That's what's wrong with this generation now. They have no respect for themselves or others." She stopped and took a deep breath. She closed the robe around her waist and tied the terrycloth belt into a tight knot to the side. She lifted her hand as if she were standing at the alter in church, summoning God's help for what she should say and do next. Then, very calmly and surprisingly lady like, she said to Tina, "Young lady, I think we got off on the wrong start. Let's try this again, shall we?"

Tina watched cautiously as the expression on my sister's face appeared to change from cold and acrimonious to one more tranquil and tempered. The assumption was that the battle had been won by the younger brawler and the old girl was about to wave the white flag of surrender after putting up a valiant, but defeated effort. That was the assumption, but we both soon discovered that our deductions were inaccurate.

Betty lowered her head, placed her left hand upon her chest, and walked up to Tina the way a nervous puppy would approach a new visitor in the house. There she stood, seemingly humbled and beaten. She lifted her head and extended her right hand in a conciliatory gesture. "Sweetheart, please forgive me," she said. "We've just met, and I've been so rude and acting very childish. Hi, my name is Sister Betty-Jean Carter, and it's so nice to meet you. Now, what did you say your name was again? Oh yes, I remember it now ..." She paused for a second or two, and that's when I knew it was coming. She picked back up where she'd left off, and the next word out of her mouth confirmed my suspicion. "Sasquatch!"

I knew it. I knew it, man. I knew it. Betty has *never* backed away from a fight, especially a war of words, insults, and insinuations. So once again, they were back at it, but this time, standing in each other's faces, yelling and screaming to the top of their lungs. I sat back in my chair, watching and waiting to see who was going to throw the first blow, and then maybe, yeah maybe (don't judge me), I'd step in and break it up. I was sure wishing I had a glass of scotch or, better yet, a tall bottle of Hennessy. Shoot, I would have settled right then for half a can of Bud Light. I mean I would have taken anything to calm my nerves. I wanted them to leave and allow me to get in my bed and sleep off this migraine that was growing by the minute, but that didn't happen. And to make matters worse, my cell phone all of a sudden started ringing.

Interrupting the unending racket with yelling of my own, I told both of them to shut up so I could answer my phone and see who was calling me. I'd left the phone in my jacket pocket that was hanging in the foyer. So I darted back down the hall and grabbed it on the fourth ring, before it went to voicemail. Already very irritated, I didn't bother or even think to look at the screen first to see who was on the other end before answering. I quickly flipped up the top and hit the answer button. "Hello?"

"Willie!" screamed the voice on the other end of the line. "Willie, is that you?"

Chapter 4: Willie's PHONE CALL

"A phone call should be a convenience to the caller, not an inconvenience to the called." ~Mokokoma Mokhonoana

THE SOUND OF HER VOICE SENT WAVES OF DREAD SURGING THROUGH my body, and I felt like somebody was wrapping barbed wire around my neck with the intention of squeezing the life out of me. I stood there immobile, wondering why I hadn't allowed voicemail to answer instead. I pride myself in never being caught off guard or allowing someone to pull a fast one on me. I mean even when I'm tore up from the floor up, I still normally manage to see a joker coming, trying to make a sucker out of me, and I stop it before it even kicks off. I don't know what happened. I guess I was just so agitated by the idiocy going on beside me that I hadn't prepared or protected myself from what was before me. *What was I thinking? Why wasn't I thinking,* was all I kept saying to myself as I tried to quickly figure out what to do. What I said next may not have been the smartest move to make, but it was all I could conjure up at the time.

"Senorita, lo siento, mucho no hablo a ingles." Now, for you non-multilingual brothers and sisters, that simply meant, "Madam, I'm sorry, I don't speak English." I had switched gears as fast as I could, going straight into my rendition of how I thought Julio Iglesias might respond. I'm sure instead of sounding like an authentic native of Madrid, I probably sounded more like a disco rap version of Ave Maria. I never took a bit of Spanish in school and truthfully, I don't even think they taught that subject in the place where I got my so-called education. My limited knowledge of this alternate dialect came from watching reruns of *I Love Lucy*. Every time Ricky got mad at Lucy, he'd start fussin' at her in Spanish, or Cubanish, or Puerto Ricanish, or whatever the doggone language was he was using. I figured if it worked for him, it might also work for me. They say that when in Rome, you do what the Romans do, but who was I kidding? This ain't Rome; this the hood. When in the hood, you do what the hood folk do; so I lied.

Betty and Tina's fussing abruptly stopped and they flipped around to see if some Mexican dude had all of a sudden burst in here and was standing in my shoes, wearing my clothes. They looked as if they didn't know if they wanted to laugh at my stupidity or run because of my insanity. They both had puzzled looks on their faces and their mouths were wide open, each paralyzed and bewildered by the way I was talking and the look of fear that had gripped me from the crown of my head to the soles of my feet. For the second time in the same morning, something had me shook. Something was crawling all over me, like the barrel of worms they had poured on that white girl on the last episode of *Fear Factor*. This time, however, it wasn't because somebody was unexpectedly in my home, rather somebody I did not want to speak with today on the other end of my phone. Somebody was calling me with an agenda, and I knew I was the object of her hostility.

The voice was brass and the tone was deep for a woman. I'd heard her speak several times recently, and normally she didn't sound like this, but it was quite obvious that she was doing her best to suppress the anxiety that was clearly building. She's been through a lot in life, and I'd made up my mind some time ago to do all in my power to help ease the pain she's been fighting for many years. She and I have history, and it's possible that we also have a future, but the way she had yelled out my name informed me that this would not be the day we'd calmly speak about what may lie ahead.

"William Alexander Prescott Lester, Jr.," the voice went on. "Don't play with me! I know that's you on this phone, tryin' to talk Spaniard and stuff! I can smell your breath all the way through this line!"

Have you ever felt like you wanted desperately to be anywhere other than where you were at the time? Has your heart rate ever sped up so fast that you thought it was going to leap out of your chest and drop to the floor in front of you? Have you ever felt your underwear start to moisten because something scared you to the point that pee starting squirting from the head of your you know what? These were a few of the experiences I had when I heard the sound of her voice again. She had called me by my entire name. I mean, who does that? The last time anyone had ever done that was when my granny had told me to bring her the switch that she was going to use to whip my behind for sucking my teeth at something she'd asked me to do. There was no avoiding this conversation; so I thought that maybe I could steer it into a direction that would result in a more pleasant outcome than what was transpiring at the moment. Maybe instead of trying to end the debate, I'd have better luck delaying it. It was worth a try.

"Mary, it's early in the morning. Listen, I just got home, I'm tired, and ain't had nothing to eat. Whatever you want, I'm sure it can wait, right?"

Yep, it was Mary, Mary Ethel Maye Stevens. The woman I'd run into at the jail last night. The woman who was once the love of my life many, many years ago. The woman who could not remember what we were to one another and what we've shared. The woman who was trapped in a place where I could not venture, and who was stuck in a realm I could not reach. The woman who was diagnosed with paranoid schizophrenia disorder many years ago and who battles today with stepping in and out of reality at the drop of a dime. The woman who spent the productive years of her life on the streets, looking for shelter under the city's bridges. The woman who fed herself with half-eaten remains people had discarded in trashcans behind restaurants and taverns. The woman who had forgotten that she bore a child many years ago—our child—the daughter I didn't know I had, the one I'd met for the first time earlier this year.

Mary had come to the jail last night with the church members to defend the pastor against the crime with which he had been charged. Several members had met earlier in the evening at the church and decided they were going to get their man of God out of lockup. I don't think any of them had a clue that I was already down there, but somehow Mary knew. You see, when they were processing me out last night, one of the guards told me that a strange looking woman had paid my bail but wanted to remain anonymous. It hadn't been too long before this when Mary had showed up at the church one Sunday morning and started attending weekly as if she'd been there all along. We've talked briefly a few times, but I always felt she didn't remember me and didn't care to discuss a past that she had no recollection of.

Anyway, let me get back to this phone call. My attempt to put it off for another time, when I was more amenable and willing to discuss my late-night revelation fell on deaf ears. Mary was not trying to work with me at all! All I asked her to do was wait a few hours and allow me to gather myself and consolidate my thoughts into a functioning format, but she was not trying to hear that. I could hear her breaths accelerate like a race car on the Indy 500 track, trying to be the first to cross the finish line. The sound she was making reminded me of that time back in the service when I attended a bullfight in Spain. I thought about how that bull saw nothing but the matador in front of him, regardless of the thousands of spectators around him. That snarling, snot-dropping beast targeted the man who was waving the red flag, and as his right hoof dug into and pushed back the dirt and rocks beneath him, he charged toward that fellow with everything he had. I could tell that Mary was feeling the same way.

"Wait?" she roared back. "No, this can't wait! I'm on my way to your place right now 'cause we got some things we gonna talk about, mista!"

I'm so glad I wasn't sucking on a brand new piece of peppermint, 'cause I'm certain I would have choked from the way I swallowed. My legs got weak and I could feel the bottom of my spine cringing and my hand tightening around the cell phone. I know this seems crazy because I've been wanting to talk to Mary for some time and try to get her to remember days gone by, but I also know that she's a wild one, and quite honestly, I was a little afraid of her these days. Here she was calling me, but I had never given her my number. And now she was coming to my house, but I had never told her where I live. This was getting scary, and I was not ready to deal with Madea's twin sister.

The two fools I already had in my house were lightweights compared to this one right here. She was broad and burley and every bit of 250 pounds. My 160-pound, thin frame was no match for this sumo wrestler in a dress. Her hands were larger than most and rough from years of life on the street, scratching and surviving the best way she could. Rumor was she once put three men in the hospital from a beat down they deserved after trying to roll her for what little money she was saving to get a winter coat from the thrift store. I bet that's the last homeless woman they ever messed with. So you can understand why I was a tad nervous about her wanting to come over here for any reason. I was more than nervous; I was down right terrified, and you could hear it in my voice.

"Mary, you're coming over here? Now, what do you want to do that for? I've already got two folk in here that I'm tryin' to get rid of. Why you think I want more company? Listen, why don't you let me get rid of these unwanted guests, and then I can take a nice, long shower, fix me something to eat and drink, and call you back so we can have us a nice, quiet conversation. Now, don't that sound good?"

Granny always taught me that you can attract more flies with honey than you can with vinegar, and Lord knows I was willing to say whatever needed to be said to convince Mary that there was no need to come to my house today. I thought if she heard the fatigue in my voice she would have some compassion, considering that I'd had a horrific night and had not been to sleep in more than twenty-four hours. Who was I misleading other than myself? I wasn't the only one whose last several hours were more than likely uneasy and unfathomable. You can't drop a bombshell on somebody like I had and think it's all right to simply walk away as if nothing happened. You can't pull somebody into a place of instability when they are barely holding on to a slice of sanity and hope that it will suddenly be all right. That, however, is what I had done to Mary.

I was guilty of unsympathetically blurting out something in public that should have been softly discussed in private between two people. She and I were now going to be affected by this announcement for the rest of our lives, and I know I should have thought it through before opening my mouth. I sat there, wondering how I would have felt if someone had disrupted my world by expecting me to believe something that was almost impossible to conceive. Some people get a kick and even make a living out of constructing shock-and-awe moments, intending, all along, to propel innocent victims into feelings of complete helplessness and depression. Some people, but not me. I didn't mean to upset her. I didn't mean to open this vault and empty out the priceless truth that could have sent her back into the dark corridors of her mind. I know it took an enormous amount of work and a lot of fervent prayers to bring her back. She was reentering a society that had forgotten about her long ago, and now, with one stupid sentence, I might have pushed my Mary back beyond anyone's reach. Instead of begging her to come and let me explain, my dumb butt told her to wait. I actually told her I wanted her to give it time and wait; however, like I said before, she wasn't having that.

"I didn't ask you what you want, and I don't care who you got over there! You better make sure you don't go nowhere 'cause you've got some explaining to do today! You got that?"

I was getting ready to adjust my tone, when the next thing I heard was silence. Uh huh … She'd hung up on me. I stood there holding the phone, shocked by the conversation we'd had. My mouth was as dry as Miss Celie's bottom lip that day that Shug Avery had kissed her in the bedroom. My teeth were rattling and shaking as if I were standing outside shoveling snow, wearing nothing but a t-shirt, basketball shorts, and flip-flops. I didn't know what to say. I didn't know what to do. I stood there motionless, looking at the wall and waiting for the angel Gabriel to come and carry me on away from here. I felt like I needed to pass gas again, but something told me that this wasn't gas trying to get out. I knew if I bent over a little bit and lifted my leg this time, I was gonna have poop running down the back of my thighs and into my shoes. So I held it in, as I'm sure you can understand.

Instinctively, I lowered the phone and slid it into my front pants pocket, and as soon as I had done that, the silence in the room was broken.

"Willie?" Betty-Jean asked, "who was that? I could hear her yelling and going off on you all the way over here."

"Sound like you 'bout to have some trouble comin' your way, my friend," Tina chimed in uninvited. "That was Mary, wasn't it, Deacon."

I turned and looked at the both of them standing there looking back at me with "stupid" written all over their foreheads. There was a tsunami swirling around in my head at this juncture and since these two were not in a hurry to leave, I decided that I would. I needed some aspirin and I wanted some liquor, but the store that carried the aspirin didn't provide the ninety-eight-percent-proof medicine that I had to have. The good thing, however, is the package store is right next door to the market. So after I made a stop at Samboes Market, you know I was going to pop my head in at Mell's Package Store. That's really what a brother had to do.

I grabbed my coat, slapped my hat back on top of my head, pulled up my britches, and tightened my belt. I informed the girls that there was no way in hell I was going to be here sober when Mary got here. I didn't know how long I was going to be gone and did not care in the least bit how long they stayed. I'm telling you I had to dip. I pulled my keys out of my right side coat pocket and opened the door.

Before I could step out into the hallway, you know who's sister yelled out one more thing. "Hey, don't forget to get some saltines. These here that you got are stale."

I couldn't do anything but wave as I pulled the door closed. I heard the two of them still talking while I locked the door behind me.

"Look, chick," Betty snarled at Tina, "I'm going back in the bedroom to finish getting dressed. Lock the door on your way out, Quanesha!"

"Wait a minute! You're not leaving me here alone to deal with another nut. I know she's unstable. The last thing I need is another old lady in my face, working my nerves!"

I turned down the hallway toward the elevators, but decided to go the other way, down the back stairs. When I got to the entrance, I heard the elevator doors open, but had no idea until later who had gotten off on my floor. I could still hear Tina and Betty fussing as I left. I understand that Tina made her move to the door to leave and go back upstairs, but just before she opened it, the doorbell rang. You won't believe who it was.

Chapter 5: Willie's SURPRISE

"Even in the familiar, there can be surprise and wonder."
~Tierney Gearon

TINA LATER TOLD ME THAT SHE STOOD LOOKING AT THE DOOR, thinking there was no way that Mary could have made it to my apartment that quickly unless she was already in the building. She'd never spoken to her, or for that matter, hardly ever spoken about her. Everyone knew about the crazy old homeless lady who lived on the streets, but no one took the time to get to know her or even find out her name. It was unlikely you would have ever seen her during the day, and the only way you might have run into her at night was if you, too, were looking through dumpsters, trying to find your next meal. It's hard to imagine that you can live for years right beside someone and not know what a valuable asset she once was to the community. It's painful to acknowledge how so many of us have walked past and stepped over the broken, battered, and beaten down, as if their lives meant nothing at all. It's sad, but it happens every day. Tina knew of Mary, but she didn't *know* Mary.

Last night was the first time Tina had actually heard Mary speak, and it was the first time she'd been in the same room with her. It hadn't even been a full year since Mary's younger sister had found her. She was doing all she could to help her return to a normal life again. Mary was with the church members who came down to the jail, trying to get Pastor Weldon out, and Tina was already in the lobby when the church members had arrived. Tina's daughter is good friends with the cop that arrested Weldon, and something about a phone call they'd had yesterday afternoon is why they were at the precinct waiting to speak with the officer. I heard that Tina watched and somewhat interacted with Mary last night. She shared with a friend of mine that she could tell that Mary still battled with mental issues, and although she was cleaned up and not looking like the street, it was clear to her that this woman was still not right.

The doorbell rang for the second time and Tina considered not opening it or saying anything at all. Maybe whoever was there would go away, thinking nobody was home. She wasn't completely sure that it was Mary standing on the other side, waiting to get in. It could have been a deliveryman or another tenant coming by to also complain about the noise. Just because Mary was the one on her mind at the moment, certainly didn't mean that she was the one out there in the hallway. It could have been anybody, but she wasn't going to take that chance today. She didn't say a word, but the person at the door did.

"Hello? Hello? Deacon Lester, are you there? It's Pastor Weldon. I need to speak to you. Hello?"

I told you that you wouldn't believe who was standing at my door. When I got back from the store and they told me who it was and everything that had gone down while I was out, I couldn't believe it. I mean of all the people in the world that I was certain would not dare bring their behinds to my front door, it was that joker right there. How in the world, why in the world would Weldon come over to see me when I had spent more time than I wanted to with him in jail last night? I had left out of the church yesterday morning 'cause I didn't want to hear him preach. I was not happy at all that the guards had put him in the cell beside mine and forced me to have to hear him whimper and whine about him being treated unfairly. As soon as they let us out, I said my piece and bolted 'cause I didn't want to deal with him or anyone else. I'll be dog footin' that somebody done told this man where I live and this morning he showed up at my apartment, saying we needed to talk. I'm glad I wasn't there because I didn't feel there was anything between him and me that needed to be discussed.

Recognizing the voice and always ready and willing to be messy and trifling, Tina immediately opened the door. With her left hand on her hip and the right one still holding the upper side of the door, she popped that gum partially dangling out of her mouth about three times really quickly and said, "Well, looky here. Look who's in my building on this early Monday morning."

For a moment there, the preacher man had seemingly lost his train of thought and the brother stood there looking back at the woman who was looking directly at him. Now to Tina's credit, even though she is as ghetto as they come, she still has a killer body. Well, that's if you like big butts and thick thighs, and I happen to be a member of that faction. I can't say for sure that the rev. was caught off guard by the figure before him, so I don't want to accuse him of that yet. It's no doubt that her curves will capture your attention, 'cause sister-girl's breasts sit up and talk to you in a language that has made many a Mandingo warrior weak in the knees. They'll do that to you, but there's also something about her demeanor that makes you a little cautious about getting mixed up with her in any way. One might assume that if you go there with Miss Tina, you might be taking on more than you or your wallet will ever be able to handle. Well ... that's what I've heard.

Anyway, it wasn't me at the door. So Rev said, "I'm sorry. I must have the wrong address. I thought this was Deacon Lester's apartment. Please excuse me but—"

"Nah, preacher, you not at the wrong address. This is Willie's place. He stepped out for a minute. I'm sure he'll be back soon. You don't recognize me, do you?"

Weldon's been at the church and in the community for a long time and he's used to people recognizing him and he not knowing or remembering them. I guess being a preacher, he knows that people will address him as if he should know who they are, especially since some of them sit before him every week, listening to what he has to say. I'm sure her face looked familiar to this idiot, since she had been in the lobby last night, but he didn't know because he don't pay attention to nobody but himself. My guess is that he stood there, poised between the decision of whether he should lie and say he recognized her, or tell the truth and confess that he didn't have a clue.

Tina saw the struggle; so she helped him out. "You may not remember me, but I'm Tina, Kalitha's mother. I was there last night when they let you out. I live upstairs, here, in the building. I decided to come down to check on Willie."

"Oh, yes, that's right. I remember you," he lied. "You said Deacon Lester will be back shortly?"

"Oh, you do remember me, huh?" She laughed. "Yeah, that's what I said. Come on in."

"I didn't realize the both of you lived in the same building, but I'm glad to know you came by to see about him."

They both walked into the living room and sat down, she on the couch and he on the chair.

"Yeah, Willie's all right. I know a lot of y'all church folk think he's an old drunk, but I've known him a long time away from the church. He's good people."

"Yes, I found that out just recently myself."

Now, I don't know why the preacher man was telling stories, and honestly I don't care. I guess he didn't want Tina to know how we felt about each other or start asking questions about what we may have talked about last night in lockup. That's what I was thinking. You know them preachers are real funny about maintaining a certain reputation among the church folk, but if he was so worried about his good name, then why was he seen going into the hotel with that girl? The cops let him go last night because they said he didn't kill that young lady, but I still want to know what he was doing in there with her in the first place. I mean how you gonna get up every Sunday, preaching about living right, praying right, serving right, and giving right, but your tail going right to the Holiday Inn Express with some chick young enough to be your daughter? That dude's a trip, but let me get back to what I understand the two of them were talking about.

"Well, preacher man, I'm glad you discovered that Willie is a good man. Make sure you tell them other holy rollers at your church the same thing."

"I will. Deacon Lester and I have been at odds for far too long, and it's time we stop bickering and fighting over crazy stuff."

"Speaking of crazy stuff, have you met his sister?"

"His sister? Deac has a sister? I'd like to meet her."

"Oh, I'm sure you'll meet her soon enough and when you do, trust me, you won't ever forget that one. Anyway, how are you doing since they let you out last night, Mr. Pastor?"

"I'm doing all right. Thanks for asking."

Tina was on the prowl, and this simpleton preacher didn't even see it coming. When this girl starts digging for information, you can bet your bottom dollar that she's going to eventually get something juicy enough to repeat at her upcoming visit to the beauty shop. She'd be a millionaire five times over if she started writing for the *National Enquirer* 'cause nobody comes up with more dirt than Tina. She was slow walking him toward the kill and no amount of seminary training could have prepared him for the hustle and flow of the street queen. It's too bad I wasn't in there to see it, but I've witnessed it many times before, so I knew where this train was headed. She kept on talking.

"Last night was a little wild, wasn't it, Preacher?"

"Last night was probably the worst night in my life. My God, I could not believe all that was happening to me. My life was falling apart, and I was about to give up hope; that is until God brought me out. Not only me, but He brought *all* of us out!"

"Oh, I'm sure you're glad to be out of that cell."

"I'm not talking about that. I'm talking about the mess our church family was in."

"Oh, you must be talking about the meeting they had on you?"

"Meeting? What meeting? What are you talking about?"

"Oh yeah, they had a hot church meeting on you last night, Rev. My girl Vickie told me all about it. Said it got krunk up in there, that folk were getting ready to fight each other. I heard some of your little girlfriends were there, looking to lynch you when they found out you was knockin' it with some young thang at the hotel."

"Girlfriends?"

"Yes, plural. Now what was that all about, Reverend? I mean, I thought a time or two about coming down to y'all's church and hear you do your thing, but if y'all up in there kickin' it like that, seem like what I need to do is keep my big butt at the house."

Without a doubt, I know Weldon wished to God that he'd kept *his* tail at home this morning. He wasn't ready for this straight out interrogation coming from somebody he didn't even know, let alone, someone who didn't even attend his church. He was probably used to people exhibiting more tact and decorum when entering into uncomfortable and unpleasant topics of conversation. He had so many flunkies around him all the time that he had been shielded from the in-your-face confrontations that are often the norm out here in the hood. You see, out here, we don't bite our tongues and we don't pull no punches because you have a fancy title and drive an expensive car. We don't care nothing about your education or the details of your portfolio, and we sure don't waste our time with cute banter and fake pleasantries. Nah, my brotha, we keep it real out here and everyone's fair game. I bet he didn't know what to say next, but Tina told me later that he stood up and gave her one of his speeches.

"I don't know what you've heard, but I don't have *girlfriends* at the church. I'm sure my members were upset from all the rumors and lies that people had obviously said about me. Now, I'm not trying to stand here and tell you that I've never done anything improper or out of line, because I have. I've done a lot of things wrong; we all have. There's not a one of us who have not sinned and fallen short of God's glory. I've got a long way to go to put things back the way they should be. I didn't come here to be hassled and verbally abused about my mistakes; I came here to talk to Deacon Lester. I'm on the right path now and I'm trying to get my life and my church back in order. So I'd appreciate it if you'd ease up on me a little bit. You know, maybe it's better that I go ahead and leave. I'll come back another time."

"Uh huh. Well, that's good, Preacher," Tina responded sarcastically. "I'm glad you found your path. Nobody should have to remain a prisoner to their past for the rest of their lives. Ain't no need for you to start stressing and gettin' your blood pressure outta whack; so calm on down before you get your little panties all in a wad. Honey, trust me, I've heard, I've seen, and I've done it all; so your little freaky rendezvous with the church girls don't move me one way or the other. Now, just sit yourself back down and be patient. I'm sure Willie won't be gone long."

Tina said that Weldon looked agitated and somewhat uncomfortable with how this conversation had turned so quickly, but also appeared very determined to follow through with his original purpose for being here. Besides, I know of several other instances when he had been under more pressure than this. Shoot, if you can't handle one woman's assertion that you're a bootleg, playboy preacher, then how are you going to help anybody fight the devil that brings it ten times harder than she does? You see, one of my issues with a lot of these preachers is that they have no problem telling us how to stand against the wickedness and wiles of the devil. They tell us to put on the whole armor of God and stuff, which is cool, and I get that. What I don't get is that when it's time for most of them to battle their own demons, it seems like they don't know how to use the right weapons of warfare. You can't keep talkin' the talk and not walk the walk. I may not be no preacher, but I know how to fight a devil.

I've been fighting one form of Beelzebub all my life and when it's time to get down and dirty with that snaggletooth liar, I gets to it. I fought that demon who had convinced my stepfather that my mother and I were his personal punching bags. I fought that monster who was supposed to be teaching me sixth-grade history, but was really trying to make me his boy toy after class in the teacher's lounge. I fought off that devil that was pushing me to shoot that white cop bastard who had pulled me over and accused me of being a drug dealer and probably stole the new car I was driving. I fought off and still fight with Legion, who sometimes creeps into my head and tries to convince me to swallow my gun, since life will never really get better anyway.

The little pressure Tina was giving Weldon was nothing. He sat there at first, not saying a word, and I can only assume that he realized he was getting worked up over nothing. Like I knew he would, he got right back to the reason for his being here.

"Miss Tina, you said earlier that Deacon Lester is a good man. He and I are leaders in the same church and we're supposed to be working as a team, but unfortunately we are not. I don't know if he's told you about our differences or if he even talks about the ministry when he gets home. If he is like me, you don't want to talk about the problems in the church when you get home from church. All you want to do is get away from the foolishness that shouldn't even be going on in God's house. Sometimes, I don't even know how we got so far away from really doing what we were both sent there to do. We've spent too many years working against each other, and it's time we work together. By the way, where did you say he went?"

"I didn't say where he went. What I said was he went out and he'll be back shortly, I guess."

I guess Tina was still flip with the preacher and didn't really care about his confessional moment at the time. She hadn't asked about our working relationship, nor did she care. She looked at her watch and realized she'd been there long enough. I was gone and my sister was in my bedroom getting dressed.

"Well, I'm sorry if my question offended you in some way, but I figured that since you were here when he left, you knew where he went."

"Do I look like his personal secretary?"

"Well, you talk like you know everything about everything, so I figured you knew where he went, but if you don't know, then don't worry about it. Forget it."

"Oh, I know where he went, preacher man. I decided that it wasn't a need for me to tell you where he went."

"Excuse me?"

"Look, I've got to go. Willie said he was going to the store to buy some things he needed. Like I said earlier, if you were paying attention, I'm sure he'll be back soon enough."

"Why are you being so rude?"

"I'm not being rude. I told you where the man went, didn't I?"

"Yeah, but you act like it was a burden on your heart to inform me—"

"I don't wanna hear no preacher jargon, my man. Save that for Sunday morning, okay? I've got to get back upstairs, but I'm sure he won't mind you being here when he gets back."

Tina was already heading to the door and walking away from Weldon as if he was boring her and getting on her nerves, when he asked, "You're leaving?"

She didn't even turn around. Ole' girl kept moving forward. "Something wrong with your hearing? I said I've got to get back to my place. I'm not staying here with you. I don't even know you. His sister's back there doing something. I'm sure she'll be out to keep you company soon enough."

"Deacon Lester's sister is here?"

She opened the door, stepped out, and as she closed it behind her, she said, "Didn't I just tell you that?"

The door closed, and Tina headed for the same back stairs that I had used earlier, but instead of going down, she went up. That fool Weldon was left standing there looking stupid like a deer in the middle of the road. He told me that after Tina left, he felt uneasy in my apartment alone. He knew my sister was back there because he could hear her doing something that sounded like singing. He realized that it wouldn't be good to be alone in someone else's apartment with a woman he didn't know.

His jacket lay on the back of the chair, where he was sitting. He'd heard his text notification go off as Tina was leaving. He took it out to see who it was. After reading the message, he grabbed his keys and got ready to leave. For some reason, he said he happened to look down on the floor and noticed that a picture had fallen from the coffee table and was partially tucked beneath the couch. He picked it up, intending to place it back on the table but was stunned by what he saw. Suddenly, he heard something outside the front door. He turned in that direction, still holding the picture in his left hand and car keys in his right. The door opened and someone walked in.

Chapter 6: Willie's SECRET

"If I maintain my silence about my secret it is my prisoner... if I let it slip from my tongue, I am ITS prisoner."
~Arthur Schopenha

It was another woman, but this one was much younger and prettier than the one who'd just left. Weldon noticed her immediately as she slowly entered, but she did not see him initially. Her iPhone gently touched her right ear and her head leaned slightly in that direction as she talked with someone on the other end. She was fully engaged in the conversation while placing her keys back inside the purse that hung over her left shoulder. She wore a simple white blouse and there was nothing spectacular about the rest of her outfit, but the purse that received her keys was, as she put it, her pride and joy.

Now personally, I don't know anything about women's pocketbooks, but later she explained to me that it was a $2,700 Pallas BB Louis Vuitton bag. She stressed that it was perfectly designed for women on the go. It gave her a sense of worth and value that old men like myself struggle to understand, but the level of importance it gave her was undeniable.

She gently closed and locked the door behind her once fully inside, and proceeded to take off her jacket while giggling on the phone. She was still unaware of Weldon's presence and a few seconds had passed before she ended the conversation and hung up. She lifted her jacket and placed it on the hook inside the foyer and began walking down the hallway toward the living room. Her head was down as she walked forward, looking primarily at her outfit and wiping away the wrinkles in her blouse.

She brushed off a small bit of lent she'd noticed on her jeans. It was clear she'd been here before and was quite comfortable with the interior layout of my apartment. She came in looking for me.

"Hello? Anybody here? Hey, I wanted to stop by and make sure you were all—"

At that moment, she lifted her head and saw Weldon standing by the couch. He was motionless and staring at her. She froze in her tracks like a Popsicle in the freezer. Neither one made a sound, as if they were puzzled about what to say or who should be the first to break the silence. The last time he was alone in a room with a young, attractive woman, it turned out to be the worst night in his life, and this felt like déjà vu all over again. Here was a man who made his living with words and who, as far as I've known, has always had something to say, even when you wished he didn't. And here was a young lady who worked nights in an environment where confidence and courage are, without question, required for success and opportunity.

A few seconds can seem like hours or even a lifetime, depending on what's before you at the time, so I understand how both of them must have been feeling. Thinking about it reminded me of a time back in Vietnam when I was pinned down and helpless, looking up into the eyes of an enemy who was positioned to take my life. I was completely out of rounds and bleeding from metal shrapnel that had ripped through my legs. My buddy and I had been running and trying to get away from pursuing gooks, when my boy stepped on a bomb in a minefield and was killed instantly. The explosion threw me over seventy-five feet and I lay there, waiting for the end to come. I always heard that your life will flash before you when the end is near, and until then, I thought it was only something the old folks said. I thought it was imaginary, but it's real. In a matter of seconds, I saw every major moment in my life. And had it not been for another soldier who took out the Viet Cong solider standing over me, it would have been my last moment.

I have to say that I do understand the feeling of shock that overtakes you when someone comes upon you unexpectedly. Shoot, when I heard Mary's voice on the phone, I swear rigor mortis started setting in as I stood there waiting on Gabriel to blow his horn. I thought my heart was about to explode and it seemed like my veins began shriveling away into the abyss. I felt the acids churning in my stomach and the room spinning faster and faster with each rotation. Running into the wrong person at the wrong time can trigger all sorts of misfires in your bodily functions.

"Oh my Lord!" Weldon said, finally ending the silence. "It's you!"

They knew of each other, but didn't really know each other. It had only been a few hours since their eyes had last met and even then, no words had been exchanged. The information she had on him and he on her was not established through personal interchange; rather, it came by way of friends and members of the street committee. It's not uncommon for people who travel in similar circles to never cross each other's paths because of differing interests. These two certainly came from and lived in different worlds, but they would soon discover that they had more in common than they ever presumed.

"You're the young lady who was at the precinct last night, aren't you?" He took one step closer to her and as he did, she took two steps backward. The edginess between them was not based in fear; instead, it was strangely uncomfortable meeting at this particular time, in this particular place. He was a guest in my home, but not invited, and she had a key to my place, but didn't live here. I'm sure both were trying to figure out why the other was there, and then the questions came. I guess that's when she decided it was a good time to make her exit.

"Oh, I'm sorry, sir. I ... I didn't see you. I came by to see ... I mean ... I only came by to speak to Mr. Lester, but I see he has company, so I'll come back later."

I can tell you, because I know this young lady well, that she did not want to be interrogated by the preacher man at all. She deals with well-known, affluent, educated, and even wealthy men all the time and those who know her know that she's not afraid of anyone or anything. She's a fighter and a survivor and prides herself on setting lofty goals and achieving them with relative ease. Her discomfort at that time was not derived from where she was or who he was, but because then was not the optimum time for a religious get-to-know-your-spiritual-co-laborer moment. She was not about to hive-five anybody and there was no confession that she needed to share with this intercessor. The preacher may be used to parishioners participating in Q&A sessions in Bible study or Sunday school class, but she was not his student or a member of the church. She had come in quickly and she'd made up her mind to leave in the same manner.

"No, wait a minute," he implored. "You don't have to rush off."

Weldon has been known to flirt with women much younger than himself, but his interest in this young lady was neither romantic or sexual. There was something about her that intrigued him and sparked his curiosity more than even he expected. Her eyes looked familiar and soothing, as if he knew the inner spirit that governed her drive and steadied her determination. She was attractive, no doubt, but not strikingly beautiful like a super model or sought after actress. There was an air about her that was infectious and her skin was as smooth as the hum of my brand new Ferrari. Well, that's if I had a new Ferrari.

He reached out to shake her hand while inviting her to take a seat so they could talk, but she had no plans to stay another minute. He didn't know her and that's the way she wanted it to stay.

"Really, that's OK. I'm gonna leave. I'll just call Mr. Lester some time later. Thank you. Have a good day."

She turned quickly and began walking back toward the door. She grabbed her jacket off the hook, put it on, and as she reached out to unlock the door, he called out. "Please don't leave, Victoria!"

Well, if you didn't already know, now you do. The young lady who had a key to my place and tried to leave undetected was my daughter, Vickie. She knew it was a possibility that the preacher had gotten a good look at her last night, but she wasn't sure since all the members had immediately run up and surrounded him the minute he'd walked into the lobby. Weldon was on the other side of the room, filling out paperwork and getting his belongings from the officer when I'd shared that bit of revelation to those close by. Honestly, I wasn't even sure he'd heard what I'd said, considering the fact that all of his girlfriends were there pampering him like he was some freakin' Arabian king or something.

She stood still, looking at the door and refused to turn and face him. Taking a deep breath, and realizing that she had been identified, she said, "What did you call me?"

"It is Victoria, isn't it? Deacon Lester's daughter? I mean, that is the name on the back of this picture I found on his floor."

She still refused to turn around and face him, though she indubitably wanted to know what picture he was referring to. She took her hands off the wall and doorknob and placed them inside the pockets of her jacket while shivering briefly as if a chill had come over her body. "I'm sorry, Pastor, but I think you may have me confused with somebody else. I'm really going to go and I'll send Mr. Lester a text message or email him later."

My baby girl held fast to her assertion, and she told me later that she desperately wanted Weldon to drop it and let her leave. That's all she wanted, but knowing him like I do, he wasn't going to let up. And I was right; he didn't. "So if I'm wrong," he maintained, "then how did you know that I was a pastor?"

This time, she turned around to address him directly while putting on the most innocent and defenseless expression she could muster. My daughter is quick on her feet and has no problem pushing back on an investigation levied against her. People have often confused her with a person they somewhat think they know because she has that face that always seems to resemble someone familiar.

"Mr. Lester invited me to the church one time and I remembered you. Anyway, my boyfriend is the police officer who arrested you in the sanctuary yesterday morning."

"Oh, is that right? Well, why don't I remember ever seeing you in church?"

"There's a lot of people in your church. I know you can't remember everybody who visits."

"Okay, I see you have an answer for everything. Well, explain something to me, if you don't mind. Why do *you* have a key to Deacon Lester's apartment?"

She didn't have an answer for that. She could deny that he'd heard what he thinks he'd heard at the jail last night, but how could she explain having a key to my apartment if she wasn't who he assumed her to be? More importantly, why were we keeping this a secret?

Weldon wouldn't stop there. "When Deacon Lester came through the door of the lobby last night, I heard what you said to him. I heard what you called him. The way you walked in here today showed me that you didn't come in expecting to speak with Mr. or Deacon Lester; you came in looking for your father."

"Listen, Pastor, you don't understand and I really don't want to talk about it right now—"

"Victoria, I heard him last night. I wasn't as far away as you might think. I know what he said to Mary and what he said in front of everybody. My question is why would a man who is so blessed with such a sweet and lovely daughter keep it hidden from everyone all of these years?"

By this time, Vickie was standing back in the living room and all she could do was slowly lower herself onto the chair and acknowledge what was said. Weldon was still holding the picture in his hand as he moved to sit down on the couch. She placed her purse on the end table and extended her hand to receive the picture he was now stretching out to give to her. It was an image of a cute little girl with long, thick black hair, tied up into two ponytails that draped evenly over the sides of her face. Her eyes were sparkling bright with excitement and her smile was as wide as Mr. Kool-Aid. She was wearing a white Polo button up shirt and a nicely pressed brown skirt that came to the middle of her knees. Her matching brown vest was adorned with an American flag pin, her troop number, a safety award pin, and three Girl Scout badges.

Vickie's eyes began to water as she held the photo in her hands. "How did he get this?"

"What do you mean? That's you, isn't it?"

"I remember when this was taken. I was away on a camping trip with the Brownies and Girl Scouts up in Redding, California. It was the summer between my fourth and fifth grade year. This was the first trip we took out of state with the troop. We went hiking way up in the mountains and fishing in some of the clearest, bluest water I've ever seen. We stayed up all night roasting marshmallows and telling ghost stories. We put makeup on each other's faces and painted our fingers and toenails when the adult scout leaders weren't watching. This was one of my fondest memories as a little girl, but I don't understand how he got this picture."

Of course Weldon didn't know anything about our family, so what she'd said surprised him. His eyebrows raised and he leaned forward, making sure to get eye-to-eye contact with her when he asked, "What do you mean? I'm sure Deac took the picture of you when you all went camping, right?"

"That's impossible!"

"What do you mean that's impossible?"

I'm sorry, but I have got to stop right here for a minute and vent before we go any further. This preacher got on my nerves when Vickie told me how he kept pushing her! I get so irritated with church paparazzi, who keep digging and digging for more information about your personal business, like they are justified in having a full account of your life's story. Anybody that knows me knows that I love the church and I like most of the church folk ... well, some of the church folk ... well, one or two of the church folk. Anyway, what crawls up my butt like a suppository searching for a hemorrhoid is when people try to disguise their nosiness as genuine concern. I mean, no matter what Vickie said, and no matter how many questions she answered, Weldon kept coming back with more.

This man thinks that because he graduated summa cum laude from some overpriced, overrated, and overbearing college, that he has the authority and clout to demand details about my baby's world. Hell, I graduated from the school of hard knocks with a come-on-soon-Lordy honor, so I guess that puts him and me on the same level, don't you think? They tell me that he worked as a family counselor back in the day and was considered one of the best in his field. That's what they say, but if he was so good, then please help me understand why he couldn't keep his family together. Why did his wife leave him and the church after fourteen years of marriage? I'd like to know where the kids are whom he should have set up with an inheritance like the Bible says a good father does. I mean he was drilling my child like she was his, and trust me, he better be glad that I wasn't back from the store at that time.

Okay, I got that out of my system. So where was I? Oh yeah, he was asking her why my taking the picture of her as a little girl was impossible.

Out of respect, she told him. "Because, Pastor, I didn't know who my father was growing up. I only met him earlier this year. I thought my biological mother and father were dead."

"Oh my God!"

"I was raised by two wonderful people in a suburb of Denver. My mother and father were incredible parents who loved me unconditionally and gave me the best they had. It wasn't until my senior year that I stumbled upon some information in my mother's office and learned I was adopted as a baby. All through school, I never thought my origin was different than what I had seen and what I had been told. Mom and Dad sat me down and told me that I'd spent the first two years of my life being raised by nuns in an orphanage in North Georgia. As a young woman, I decided to find out who these nuns were and where I was born. My mother was going to travel with me to Atlanta and help me gather information, but my father was suddenly taken from us in a car accident two months before we planned to go. We were devastated. Mom took it worse than me. He meant

91

everything to her and she never worked outside the home. She needed me more than ever, so I decided to drop it. I decided to leave it alone. I thought it was out of my system, but it wasn't."

"How did you find out? I mean what did you do?"

"Eventually, I wanted to know my real name and who my biological parents were. I wanted to know why they didn't keep me. I couldn't understand why they gave me away to strangers. Did they not love me? Did they ever even try to find out where I was and what happened to me? Did I have brothers and sisters out there that I knew nothing about? Why did my parents keep this hidden from me and why did God take my father from me before I could learn the truth? I had a lot of questions, but Mom didn't want to talk about it with me. She was offended that I would ask about parents who had abandoned her. She had changed, but I still needed to know. I had questions but no answers.

Well, I finally decided to make the trip and find these nuns. I not only traveled out here, but I moved out here. When I go after something, I press hard to get it. I don't let anything or anyone stand in my way. I found the orphanage and I started asking the nuns and workers there if any of them remembered me. When I asked how I ended up in the home they said they couldn't tell me. I didn't buy that, so I kept pushing. Later, I received a letter in the mail saying that my biological mother had died a few weeks after I had arrived at the home. The letter also stated that the orphanage didn't know the circumstances surrounding her death. I still don't know if I believe them, but that's all the information I could get."

"I'm so sorry you had it rough growing up and I deeply sympathize with you. I can't begin to imagine the other challenges you must have faced and the many obstacles you had to deal with. I'm sure things were tough and some days you probably didn't know what to do, but look how well you've turned out! It's obvious that God had His hand on you and—"

"God? Excuse me, Pastor, no offense, but don't start preaching to me this morning about your God. As far as I'm concerned, there *is* no God!"

Weldon slid all the way up to the front of the couch. The look of compassion he previously held was now bewilderment. He couldn't believe what he'd heard, and honestly, when I found out what she had said, I couldn't either. I know I'm far from the perfect example of what a Christian is supposed to be and I was nowhere around during Vickie's formidable years. And I'm not sure if those people who raised her even took her to church as a little girl, but no matter what I've been through and no matter what I've seen, I've always known that God was real. Even before my granny really taught me how to pray, I'm telling you I knew God was real. Maybe during all those nights when I heard my mother calling out to God for help when her husband was abusing her I began to believe. Some people may say that if there was a God watching over her, He wouldn't have allowed her to be beaten night after night. I just looked at it a different way. I felt that the only reason this evil man who was beating my mother didn't kill her is because God wouldn't allow him to take her life. He protected her, even in the worst of times.

Weldon was caught off guard by Vickie's admission. All he could say was, "Hold on a minute, young lady. What do you mean God is not—"

"No, you hold on a minute!" she shouted back, standing up and shaking her neck and pointing her finger. "Don't try to tell me about a so-called loving God! Because if there were such a thing, He wouldn't leave so many kids abandoned and alone in a home full of strangers! Don't come preaching to me about a God who supplies all of your needs 'cause, Preacher, I've been the supplier of my needs for a long time! I moved out here looking for answers and all I ran into was pain and disappointment! I couldn't hold down a decent job and at times had nowhere to live! I did what I had to do to make it. I had to make ends meet and stay off the streets by any means necessary. This body and these brains are what got me through!"

"Victoria, I had no idea that we would run into each other today. Twenty-four hours ago, I didn't even know if I would see the light of day again, but our meeting in this place, at this time ... this *is* God! Now again, I know you've had it rough, but—"

"You know? You know? Preacher, you don't know me! You don't know *anything* about me! Do you know that I am a dancer? Do you know that I take off my clothes on stage for crusty, sick, nasty men, who try to grab at my vagina when they slip money into my G-string? Do you know the nights I had to spend with disgusting, degenerate, dysfunctional old geezers like you in order to make enough money to eat? Do you know that the girl you were with in the hotel that night was my best friend?"

Weldon's eyes popped wide open and he felt like he was about to swallow his tongue. The room went black for a second and then started spinning rapidly in a counter clockwise direction. His mouth became bone dry and his heart rate began beating at an accelerated pace. He was trying to respond, but the words would not come out. Vickie knew she'd hit a nerve and normally she would have let it go, but she felt he deserved this.

"Yeah," she continued, "the one that ended up dead! The one they accused you of murdering!"

"B-b-but I didn't—"

"Yeah, I know you didn't do it, but you had no business being there with her, did you, preacher man? Let me ask you something: Did you take the time to pray with her? Did you read the Bible to her and explain the profound scriptures and parables in the New Testament to her? Did you tell her about your God and all He's done for her life? Did you even know she was a pastor's daughter? Did you know she had a little boy who's now going to grow up without a mother? No, I'm sure you didn't know any of that. You weren't there to talk to her about any of those things, were you? You weren't there to talk about your God to her then, so don't start trying to tell me about your God now!"

Weldon's head dropped between his shoulders and he slumped back onto the couch as if a five-thousand-pound boulder were sitting on his chest. I bet he was wondering how he ended up this far away from the will of God and how he'd left a little boy without a mother.

"Victoria, I ... I'm. Oh God, I'm so sorry. I made so many mistakes. Again, I had no idea—"

"You're right; you don't have any idea! You know, on second thought, maybe it is good that you're here. We will sit here together and wait on my father to get back. I've got a lot of questions that need to be answered today. A lot of questions!"

Weldon was just about to say something else, but before he could, somebody kicked open my door.

"Willie!" Mary yelled as she burst in.

Chapter 7: Willie's NEIGHBORHOOD

"The world has narrowed into a neighborhood before it has broadened into a brotherhood." ~Lyndon B. Johnson

I TOLD YOU EARLIER THAT WHEN I GOT OFF THE PHONE WITH MARY, after she'd informed me that she was on the way over, I left my place as fast as I could. There was no way that I was going to be anywhere around when she showed up. They had told me how loud and out of control she was acting at the church meeting yesterday. One minute, she was talking like she had some sense, and the next, they said she was freakin' out like she was from another planet, or something. I know it's true because I heard her myself going ham upstairs in the jail lobby while I was down in my cell. Her voice had come through the vent as clearly as if she were standing right beside me. She was yelling and fussing about some of everything and it was pointless for anyone to try to get a word in edgewise. When Mary's mind was made up and she started raging, the best thing anyone could do was quickly shut up and let her get it out of her system.

This morning, I had tried everything I could to convince her there was no need to come visit me today, but when that came to no avail, a brother got ghost. I was hoping that by the time I got back, Tina and Betty-Jean would be gone and my home would be quiet and empty. I don't have the most elaborate apartment in the world, but it's mine, all mine. Nobody lives with me, and that is absolutely the way I like it. If I came through my door and kicked off my shoes in the living room, I didn't have to deal with anyone telling me to take them to my room and put them in the closet. If I plopped down on the couch, grabbed the remote control, flipped on the TV, unbuttoned my pants, and scratched my sack, I didn't have to worry about anybody saying that I was being mannish. If I wanted to sit buck naked at the table and eat Vienna sausages and crackers while drinking beer and passing gas, I could do it because this was my crib. If I felt like shooting a booger across the room by pressing down on one side of my nostril and blowing hard out of the other, then I could and I wouldn't have to hear anybody tell me I'm nasty. Now, I understand that Luther had said, "A house is not a home when there's no one there to hold you tight," but I did not want anybody in my house, holding nothing.

When I had started walking down those back stairs, I knew there were two people in my place, but I had no idea that by the time I made it out of my building, there would be three. I didn't know that while I was making my way out, Weldon was making his way in. Oh well, I couldn't worry about what was happening upstairs. I had to get as far away from the commotion as I could. I had walked fourteen flights down the back stairs of my building and left Tina and Betty-Jean inside to finish whatever debate they were having. The stairwell in my building is supposed to be well lit so that those who use it don't accidentally trip over something that may be lying on the floor. It's supposed to be that way, but it wasn't. The few light bulbs there were not illuminating the area well at all. Some genius had the bright idea to replace the one-hundred-watt bulbs with forty-watt bulbs instead, which I guess had to be the cheap landlord who was always cutting corners to save a buck. It was also a little cold in there, which I didn't mind. I mean I expected that, but what I didn't anticipate was opening the door and running straight into the funk that hit me and almost knocked me back.

I don't even know the best way to describe it other than to tell you that it was a mixture of feet, armpits, bad breath, pee, marijuana, moonshine, vomit, and booty. The floor was sticky and the walls were greasy, but who in the hell had tossed their baby's dirty, boo-boo-filled diaper in here. That's what I really couldn't understand. Do you know how pissed I would have been had I accidentally stepped in that? Oh my God, I would have cussed everything and everybody out in this entire building had I tripped over that and got some on my Stacy Adams.

Oh, wait a minute. I almost forgot to tell you this: I was a little more than halfway down, when this fool came bursting into the stairwell, waving a pocketknife, telling me to give him my money. I really felt bad for this idiot because he didn't realize who he was screwing with. I wish somebody would have told him that I was the last person in the world he wanted to try and rob with a ridiculous pocketknife. This crackhead jumped out at me, wearing a black Ninja Turtles outfit, yelling like Steve Urkel on *Family Matters*. I'm not a big guy myself, but he couldn't have been more than ninety pounds soaking wet. His hands were shaking, he had holes in his shoes, and his lips were so chapped and white. He had no idea that I had killed more men in Vietnam than he'd killed cockroaches and water bugs in the drug house. I almost hated to have to put this full-grown ass whippin' on him, but trust me, it so had to be done. So I did it.

I stepped over him and left him moaning and lying on the floor next to the dirty diaper and a half-eaten Taco Bell burrito, of which he was eating (at least I hope it was the burrito he was eating and not road kill). Oh well, I had finally made it to the bottom floor and pushed on the door to get out. I walked outside and was met by the rays of the morning sun, which caused me to close my eyes quickly for a second until they adjusted to the brightness. I opened them in time to see a football coming straight for my head. I ducked before it could pelt me and heard it hit the brick wall and fall to the pavement.

"Sorry, Mr. Lester," I heard from P.J., who was one of the few respectful boys always playing football in the parking lot behind the building. A bunch of them were out there talking trash and cussing, with no concern for anyone but themselves. All of these boys thought they were going to be the next NFL superstars and sign multimillion-dollar contracts. They said they were going to live up on the north side of town and hang out with the rich white folk and date their daughters. I guess it didn't dawn on them that first you had to go to school and pass more than your P.E. class in order to advance to college and then into professional sports. Others had done it and risen from the brokenness and poverty of the ghetto, but those who got out were definitely the minority, not the majority. I'm not about killing nobody's dreams, but success requires more than desire; it also takes a whole lot of discipline. You can't be drinking Hennessy and smokin' reefer every day and then think you can push your body up and down a football field for four quarters. You can't be hustling on the street and banging all night long if you expect to be productive at two-a-day practices that most high school coaches consider a basic norm during pre-season training. These young cats have the talent, but I really wonder how many of them understand the work ethic that's required to excel to the top level.

It felt good being back outside again, even though it hadn't been that long since I'd been out there. It was a clear day and there was barely a cloud in the sky. I wish I could tell you that the birds were singing cheerfully in the trees, but you've got to have trees first in order to have birds singing in them. Shoot, not only did we not have trees, but we didn't have green grass to walk on or even bushes to hide your beer cans behind. Nah, the only thing around here that was green, was the graffiti on the wall that one of the gang boys had painted up there six months ago. We had concrete and weeds, and even the weeds didn't look healthy. My block had changed a lot from what it was the first day I'd stepped foot on it, but I still loved her and she loved me. I spent more time in this hood than anywhere else in my life. I met my wife out here. My daughter was born in the hospital down the street from here. The funeral director who had embalmed my bride and baby girl lives in a house less than a mile from here. The cemetery that's holding their bodies right now is just south of here. It's been hard at times, but I decided a long time ago, I would always be here.

As I began to head toward the sidewalk, I turned and looked back up at my building, wondering what was going on inside my house. Were my sister and neighbor still going at each other full steam, or had they calmed down and called it a draw? Was the guy who lived directly below me still curling the hair and painting the toenails of the guy who lived across the hall from me, since that was their routine every Monday morning for the past six weeks? I saw some sheets hanging out of one of the ninth-floor windows. They probably should have been hung there to dry after they'd been washed; instead, somebody had hung them outside to air out. How did I know, you ask? Well, I saw the big yellow piss stain slap dab in the middle of the white sheet as it waved and flapped in the wind. But there was nothing as funny as watching Ms. Jenson and her boyfriend knocking boots up against the window on the fourth floor. I'm not just an old man, but I'm a dirty old man, and normally I'd enjoy a little sexual exhibition, but when both participants are in their early eighties, it's just nasty.

I'd seen enough, so I turned back around and got ready to make my way up the street to my favorite little corner store. The market had been in this community longer than I'd been here and you could always find what you needed when you walked inside. It was several blocks away, so I knew it was gonna take me a little time to get there and back, but I was in no hurry. I didn't care how far away it was. The walk would be good for me. I'd have time to clear my mind and figure out what I was going to say to Mary if she was there when I got back. I also needed to come up with a plan to get Betty-Jean out of my house, 'cause I was not trying to put up with her shenanigans today.

I had no sooner moved twenty feet up the sidewalk, than I heard the sound of a siren behind me. It wasn't unusual to hear or see the police in the neighborhood. Most of the black cops on the force grew up around here and they still had families and girlfriends who lived in the area. If they weren't rushing to a call, then they were patrolling the streets. So I didn't even turn around to see what the deal was until I heard somebody call my name.

"Hey, Willie, what you doing out her, man?"

I turned around to see Officer Raylon Jackson, who had pulled up beside me in the patrol car.

"Raylon, what you doing out here? Didn't I just see you last night? Don't you ever sleep? I don't remember the last time I saw you in something other than your uniform."

"Hey, Shamika!" he yelled at one of the young female tenants who had just walked out of the building next to mine. "Get that little nappy headed boy of yours back in the house and put some clothes on him! He standing out here sucking on that stupid pacifier in nothing but his pampers! And change the one he's got on now! The front of them is as yellow as the damn school bus, girl!"

She flipped him off as she picked up her son and yelled something back at him, but I couldn't make out what she'd said. He laughed and shot her the bird right back. "Trick, don't make me come put you in the back of this car and haul your lazy butt downtown again."

I immediately redirected his attention back to the conversation that we were having before he was distracted by the girl and her half-naked baby. "Raylon, stop harassing her. You know she's not bothering nobody."

"Man, Willie, I don't know if our people ever gonna act like they got some sense around here. I'm tired of locking up our people over and over again, but some of them just don't get it."

He gave me that look as if I was a part of that crowd who didn't get it. He thought he knew me and everybody else in the neighborhood, but if truth be told, I knew this young guy more than he knew himself. You see, I watched him grow up around here and was well acquainted with his father back in the day. His dad worked at the mill and from the outside, it seemed as if he had the respect of his co-workers and supervisors. That's how it appeared, but those of us who lived in the hood knew that he was really just a prick and a pathetic excuse for a man. This dude never really cared about or had time for his kids. I guess it's hard to make time for fifteen children from nine different women, especially when you've never even tried to learn their names. He made good money at the plant, but would hardly give a dime to his kids or any of their mothers. He walked with a limp from blowing out his knee, playing street ball in his early twenties. His nine-to-five was only a way to shield the authorities from how he really made his money. You see, he was nothing more than a hustler and a pimp. He lived hard and had died the same way. Raylon's old man had owed some guys some money, and when he didn't pay up, they shot him down in the street like a dog. Raylon was no more than eight years old when he saw this happen right there before his own eyes. I'm sure that it shook him to the core. It's hard enough for a child to get over experiencing violence and death of any kind, but when it's somebody you care about, it can destroy you. However, in Raylon's case, it motivated him to be the exact opposite of his father.

Initially, he hung out on the streets and tried to act hard like the other little thugs whose future seemed no brighter than his dad's. There was always a group of immature, impressionable boys, who were nothing more than pawns and flunkies for the drug dealers who used them as lookouts and runners. I knew how the game was played and I watched so many of these kids get drawn into a dead end existence, where their epilogue would be a prison term of twenty to life or their bodies lying on a slab in the county morgue. Young Raylon was on his way to that same fate had it not been for his grandmother, who stayed on him and prayed over him every day of her life. She reminded me of my granny by the way she would plead the blood of Jesus over him and do whatever she had to in order to save him from the streets. It couldn't have been more than a year after his father's death that she sent him somewhere up north to get him away from all of this madness. When he finally returned, about twelve or so years later, he still had attitude and a chip on his shoulder, but now he was a man, working for the man.

"Raylon, had it not been for your grandmother and family that loved you and looked out for you, you'd be riding in the back of this car instead of driving it."

"Old man, you ain't never lied. I know I was nothing but a young fathead, running around here making drop offs for Sly and his crew. Yeah, that was crazy. All them cats are dead now and still, these young soldiers ain't got a clue that slinging this crap is pointless."

The dispatcher's voice abruptly interrupted our conversation. *"All units! All units! Signal sixty-three at M.L. King and Hightower!"* Normally, the dispatcher would repeat the incoming call before the patrolman responded, but everyone knew that signal sixty-three meant that an officer was in serious trouble and needed help right away. Raylon just pulled the gearshift into drive and took off down the road without saying another word. It's a good thing that I wasn't leaning inside the window talking to him, rather standing a few feet back on the sidewalk. I watched as he sped down the road and whipped a screeching right turn at the corner, heading south. I lifted my right hand and asked God to protect him and his comrade in whatever trouble had befallen him. I looked back at the building behind me one more time to see that the little half-naked boy was back outside the door again, sucking on that same pacifier and playing in the dirt. I just chuckled and shook my head as I recommenced my journey to the store.

Regardless of how old you get, there are some things we do that take us back to the days of our youth. As I walked along, I remembered the game we used to play as kids coming home from elementary school. There I was, smiling and giggling, while making sure that I didn't step on a crack and break my mama's back. It had been a long time since I'd ventured out for a morning stroll in an effort to eliminate the crazy concerns and issues that were going on in my world. For a moment there, I'd literally forgotten about the theatrics between Tina and Betty-Jean going on in my apartment. I was no longer thinking about Mary and what she wanted to talk about. My time in jail last evening now seemed more like a movie I had watched on a late-night cable channel than something I had actually experienced. I just jumped and skipped over every crack, line, or word that was written into the concrete beneath my feet. It didn't matter that I couldn't move as quickly or jump as high as I used to. All that mattered was that the sun was shinning, the dogs were barking, this old heart was beating, and an old man's legs were feeling no pain.

"Willie." A woman's voice suddenly broke my concentration. "What in the world are you doing over there?"

I looked up and realized that I had made it to the next block on my journey and was being watched by one of the members of the church, who was the definition of a neighborhood busy body. Gail was sitting out on her porch, eating what appeared to be a scrambled egg and tomato sandwich and sipping on a cup of coffee. I believe she and I are around the same age and we've both been a part of the church and this community for about the same length of time. She never married, but her live-in boyfriend passed away I'd say about ten or eleven years ago. He was a tall, quiet gentleman who really didn't talk much, but that's because he lived with a woman who didn't make room for anyone else to ever get a word in, if you know what I mean.

She is an usher at the church and has worn that same white blouse, black skirt, and them Payless, safeTstep, clog-looking black shoes every Sunday for the last umpteen years, or it seemed like it to me. I understand that her mama was an usher, her grandmama was an usher, two of her aunts were ushers, three of her five sisters are ushers, her two brothers both married ushers, her daughter is an usher, and hell, her last dog, before he died, was probably an usher too. I feel you needed to know that because you know sometimes ushers are used to telling everybody where to sit and what to do, so she thinks that out here, away from church, she can do the same thing. As soon as I heard her voice, it reminded me of why I normally catch a cab to the store or ride with my buddy when he goes. I'm not going to say that Gail is the reason why I have a drink or two most every day, but she was the reason I bought an extra bottle today. Once she starts going, it can last forever.

"Deacon," she continued, "I didn't see you at the church meeting last night. You know Pastor done went and got himself into some trouble here again. They said it's about some fast little girl young enough to be his daughter. If you mens would one day learn to keep your little taliwackers in your pants and think with your brains instead of your you know what, then you wouldn't be getting in trouble all the time. These young ones running around here grabbin' on their crotches, tryin' to keep they pants from falling down, and you old ones think your blue pill gonna help you get back some of your youth again. Shoot, most of y'all don't even know what to do with it when you get it. That old fool I had was always doing it wrong and when he finally got it right, he fell asleep before I could get to where I was tryin' to get to."

I couldn't do anything but stand there with a dumb look on my face, trying so hard not to get the visual of her and her old man together. I didn't want that impression in my mind, but dang it, it was too late. It was there and she was still talking.

"So tell me, what Pastor done did? I know you know since you been trying to get him outta there all these years. You need to just leave that man alone and stop drinking like a fish all the time. You smelled like a liquor house yesterday, up there leading devotion and making everybody on the front row dizzy when you opened your mouth. You probably going to the package store now, aren't you? Don't you know that's not the type of example you supposed to be setting for these young folk out here? You deacons are supposed to be taking care of the church and peoples, but all y'all wanna do is control the money and tell the pastor what he can and can't do. Lord, if my granddaddy were alive he'd slap the tar-ba-Jesus off of all y'all, the way y'all be letting the church go down! Now, he was a true deacon, a real deacon. You know he helped Rev. McMichael start this church. My papa was a brick mason and he laid the bricks on this church one by one. That was back when mens worked hard and took care of they families and knew how to pray and lead devotion."

While she was going on and on, I leaned on the outside of her fence, trying my best to get a word in, but it didn't work. I swear she is so much like my sister, and no matter what I tried, she was not going to stop talking until she got everything out of her system. I could handle her babbling at one hundred miles a minute, I was used to that. I've seen her eat some of the craziest combinations of food you could think of, but that don't bother me much either. However, there is one thing she did that almost made me hurl what little bit I had in my stomach. Some years back, old gal here used to be a two-pack-a-day smoker, until the doctor told her that if she didn't stop she would be shaking hands with St. Peter. So she went from smoking hand rolled bali shag cigarettes, to chewing and spitting Skoal Wintergreen snuff. Do you *not* understand how absolutely disgusting it is to watch an old woman chew and spit tobacco? Father God, the stuff that this woman was spewing out of her mouth was the grossest lump of snuff I'd ever seen. It was thick, long, and sticky when it hit the ground. Can you imagine seeing a lumpy black mixture of chewed up dip, yellow eggs, and red tomato sauce flying into the air in your direction? I honestly don't even know why I stopped and gave her any of my time and attention when she'd called my name. I should have known that she was going to upset my stomach. Hell, now I was gonna have to add an economy-size bottle of Pepto-Bismol to the grocery list.

I had to go, and I mean I had to get the devil out of there right then. After my encounter with the human regurgitating machine, I'd lost all interest in the game on the sidewalk that I was having so much fun playing. My focus was shot and my nerves were bad. Thankfully, I was able to quickly remind myself of the original mission at hand. The mission, my dear brothers and sisters, was to secure a much-needed liquid nourishment as quickly as I possibly could. I turned back around and started to leave, but almost tripped over something. I looked down and realized that one of my shoes was untied, so after bending down and getting it straight, I took up my trek to the local corner store again.

I had to do something to free my thoughts from the gunk that Gail had just spit onto the ground before me, and the only thing I could come up with to unshackle my soul was to sing. These days, I only sing in church during devotion service or during the few times when the choir goes back and sings one of those good old James Cleveland or Andre Crouch numbers. Most people don't know this, but when I was overseas in the service, I used to sing at nightclubs on the weekends to make a little extra money. My boys and I had a group called the Super-Fly Soldier Boys and the ladies loved us. I would sing lead most of the time, unless I felt like playing my saxophone instead. That's when I'd let one of the younger cats work on his vocals and swoon his way into the arms of a naïve local girl. Some people said I had a voice like Nat King Cole. We weren't singing church songs back then. Oh no, the stuff we were laying down would get you run out of the church back in those days. Man, I miss those days.

Just as I was about to start singing my third number, I looked up and I was there. I'd made it. I grabbed my wallet from my back pocket, opened the door, and walked in.

Chapter 8: Willie's HEADACHE

"If you have a lot of tension and you get a headache, do what it says on the aspirin bottle: 'Take two pills' and keep away from your ex." ~Unknown

I BELIEVE THAT AROUND THE SAME TIME I WAS WALKING INTO THE corner store, Mary was kicking in my apartment door ...

"All right, all right, where is he? I mean *where is he?* Where is that beer-drinking, pigeon-toed, big-lip, lazy-eye, dirty, old, good-for-nuthin', lying, wannabe deacon?"

They tell me that when she came through that door it sounded like a fully loaded freight train flying down the track at ninety miles an hour, slamming into the side of a nuclear power plant. When that door swung open, it hit the back wall with such force that it knocked all of my pictures to the floor. In one swoop, she'd shattered the frame my granny had given me before I went off to join the Marines. I guess she thought she was SWAT or a part of the full tactical division of the DEA. Mary came busting into my place as if she were there to break up an international drug ring. Who did she think was up in there? It didn't make no sense the way that woman charged in there, yelling and fussing to the top of her lungs. I did not appreciate the damage done to my door either, and you already know I was stuck with the repair bill.

I would have loved to see the reaction on Weldon's face when that cyclone in stockings rushed in. I would have fallen straight to the floor and laughed until snot came out of my nose. Vickie said Mary scared the fool out of him. The two were still sitting down talking the moment she came crashing in. He jumped up screaming like someone was popping a big pimple on the side of his nose or something. I bet that preacher wet his pants too. He won't ever admit it, but the way he whimpered and cried in that cell last night convinced me that he was nothing more than a big old chicken. He's always telling us to be strong in the Lord and put on the whole armor of God and stuff. Always quoting that scripture, "If God be for you, He's more than the whole world against you." Well, it didn't sound like he thought that God was big enough to handle my baby's mama coming through that door.

Mary was so bent on getting to me that she didn't even realize who were all in the apartment. It took a second for Weldon to figure out who it was, so after he climbed down off my couch, he walked back down the hallway to where Mary was standing and tried to calm her down.

"Sister Mary, what in the world are you doing? Now listen, you've got to take a seat and calm down so we can talk about—"

"Calm down? Calm down? Reverend Pastor, don't you dare tell me to calm down! You calm down! I told that man that I was on my way over here and he was not to go nowhere!"

"You mean Deacon Lester?"

"Well, who else in the devil would I be talking 'bout?"

"Sister Mary, if you're looking for Deacon Lester, I understand that he'll be back in a minute. He wasn't here when I arrived either, but they told me he went down to the—"

Before he could finish, she cut him off again. Mary did not win the Miss Congeniality contest in high school, so being respectful and cordial while conversing with others was not her forte. When I knew her back in the day, she was a very warm and loving woman, but she had a rough side too. That's not uncommon for most of us. I know we all try to treat our fellow man with dignity and respect, but if someone pushes the wrong button, there's no telling what spirit will rise up. My revelation last night, in conjunction with our phone call this morning, must have awakened that spirit in her. Weldon had no idea that when Mary makes up her mind about something, there's no reasoning with her. You can't reason with someone who's not sure from one minute to the next in what world she's operating anyway.

"I'm an upstanding, God-fearing, law-abiding Christian woman! And do you know what that man has done? Well, do you?"

"Sis Stevens, I see that you're upset and maybe if we take a moment and start from the beginning, I'm sure we'll find a happy—"

"Upset? Upset! I'm *way* past upset! My name has been soiled and my integrity questioned!"

All of a sudden, without any warning or provocation, she broke out into song. "I have been 'buked, scorned, talked about as sure as you're born. I've been up, down, level to the ground! Long as I got King Jesus … long as I got King Jesus … long, long, long as I got Him, I don't need nobody else!"

Weldon stood there wondering what in the world he was witnessing. He'd had a few encounters with Mary in the past and I understand that she even walked into the sanctuary one Sunday morning and did her thing in E-flat. I mean, old girl was wearing one of his robes and preaching to the empty pews a few hours before church service began. They tell me she had a cordless mic in one hand, a miniature Bible in the other, one of his monogramed towels draped over her shoulder, and a crystal glass of milk on the book board. She wasn't merely expounding on a text, she was squalling and tuning like the good old Baptist boys do on the closing night of a revival meeting. As she was going in, she would put the Bible down to the side and wipe sweat pellets off her brow with the towel. She moved back and forth across the pulpit, making sure that she spoke directly to every invisible parishioner in the house. I bet she even told whatever congregation she saw in her mind to high-five their neighbor. So now, there she was, standing by the door in the hallway, singing and lifting her hands to the Lord.

"Please tell me," Weldon interrupted, "you're not going to keep singing and hurting my ears all morning, are you?"

As quickly as she'd started singing, she stopped. Then she turned and looked up toward the corner of the room as if she saw something or someone attached to the wall. Her eyes were fixed on an area approximately thirty-six inches below the ceiling and over to the right of a clock I have hanging there. She was mumbling something to herself, but Weldon couldn't make out what it was. Suddenly, she spoke up and said, "I need justice, do you hear me? I've been lied on and I need some justice in this world! Somebody get Judge Judy in here 'cause I've been wronged!"

These types of outbursts went on for several minutes as Weldon cautiously stood back and watched in amazement and awe. Vickie was already irritated by Pastor, so she was not trying to help him figure out what Mary was saying and doing. One minute she was calm and collected, with no signs of mental disorders or dysfunction, and the next she was rambling on and jumping from one subject to the other. As he watched her, he could tell that she was by no means ignorant or uneducated. To his surprise, she was very knowledgeable about a lot of things. She was philosophical about life in general and her theology was dead on accurate. She would speak about current events in great detail and was even more precise with historical facts and references. He wondered how could a person be so connected and disconnected at the same time. Then he thought about himself.

How could a man be so dedicated to advancing the Word of God, but struggle to maintain a faithful and upright walk in that same God? How could a man in thirty minutes of preaching describe the principles of Christianity with such precision and poise, but fail in over thirty years to subdue a reoccurring demon of lust that altered his conduct. He thought about what Vickie had told him earlier about her friend and what they meant to each other. How did he not know that she was a pastor's daughter? How would he feel if he had a daughter and a man his age became intimately involved with her? More importantly, why did he not treat her as the precious child of God that she was? Watching Mary go back and forth, in and out, caused him to confront the instability that he wrestled with every day.

His thoughts were interrupted as her noticeable agitation intensified. He said, "Sis Mary, I think we really need to sit down and talk, and I'm sure we will all see that—"

"Ain't no time for sitting down! Oh no! It's time to give somebody an old-fashioned, country whoopin'! Do you know that that man done went and told everybody dat we is havin' relations? Well, do you?"

"Relations" is the term that the mothers in the old apostolic Pentecostal church would say when referring to two people having sex. I guess it sounded better. However you say it, Mary was not happy at all that I'd left everyone with that impression. She didn't stop there.

"He must have taken advantage of me when I was in a vulnerable state! Oh Lord, it's so hard, so very hard fighting off all these men! God, why did you bless me with so much beauty?"

"Huh?" is all Weldon could say.

See, back in the day, Mary was as fine as silk cotton and had a body as sweet as a Snickers bar, or that's what I thought. I'll never forget the first time I saw her in that killer blue dress, toting that cute matching little purse. Now, I can't remember what time of day it was or if the sun was shining or not. I don't remember what type of car I was driving or what street corner we were close to. I can't even tell you if it was winter, spring, summer, or fall, because the moment I saw her, everything else went blank. Her skin was flawless and her eyes were spectacular. I was drawn to her and knew the second I saw her that I had to find out her name. She was amazing and I knew, deep beneath the layers of misery that the streets had dished out to her, there was still a diva somewhere inside. Time had taken a toll on all of us, but Mary's life had been dark these many years. It was hard for others to see the beauty that I once knew so well.

"I don't bother nobody, Lord!" she continued. "I reads my Bible and I pays my dues! I'm a good girl, merciful Savior, and I gives to the poor. Well, I gives to me, and that's the same thing."

"Sis Mary, the Lord knows you've been faithful to Him, and He's going to work things out for you. I mean I really feel that if we could take a seat over here and …"

He'd almost finished his sentence, but I guess he was talking too slowly. There was another song brewing in her belly, and it just had to come out. "Some folk would rather have houses and lands. Some folk choose silver and gold. These things that dey treasure and forget about their soul … but I've decided to make Jesus my choice!"

Weldon rolled his eyes and dropped his head between the palms of his hands. He thought choir rehearsal was over. He stood there quietly and did not try to interrupt her this time. After she sang all four verses and the chorus twice, she was done. He got ready to invite her again to the living room to talk, but before he could, she hit him dead in the chest with her pocketbook.

"And don't think you can have your way with me neither, mister. I am *not* that kind of woman!"

"Say what?" he said, clutching his chest and gasping for air.

"I saw the way you was looking at me, undressing me with dem beady eyes. And I don't care what promises you make to me; if you like it, then you gotta put a ring on it! Oh oh oh!"

It sounded like things were getting a little crazy up in there, but it was about to be crazy to the tenth power. The bedroom door swung open, and out walked the one and only Betty-Jean Carter in the flesh.

"What in the Sam hell is going on out here? And who in the devil are all you people?"

Vickie said Betty came out of that room looking around like she was about to crack some watermelons over the heads of everybody in her vicinity. She said her expression looked exactly like Sofia's when she'd knocked Miss Millie's husband flat out after he'd slapped her in the face in front of her two children. I told you my sister always had a mouth on her, but I failed to inform you that she was known for fighting anybody at the drop of a hat. It had to be God, the angels, and sweet Baby Jesus Himself who kept her from uppercutting Tina when she got all up in her face this morning. I have watched my sister fight a slew of girls at the same time, boys, men, teachers, police, and even street thugs. I prayed that she had mellowed through the years and was thankful to God that my apartment wasn't destroyed by the things and people she would have thrown around. I honestly think that some of her husbands had left her because they got tired of getting beat on when they tried to voice their opinion or disapproval about something she'd said or done.

Betty had exchanged the white terry cloth robe she had been wearing earlier for a purple and orange dress she'd apparently brought with her. Yes, she'd taken off my robe, thank you Jesus, but she was still wearing my brand new slippers. My bedroom door is right down the hall from the living room, so when she heard Mary and the preacher, that was the first room she entered. When the two of them heard her voice, they, too, entered the living room, where Vickie was still sitting quietly on the couch, filing her nails and watching the drama unfold. The three of them entered the living room at the exact same time, and as Weldon was extending his hand to meet and introduce himself to my sister, Mary saw Vickie.

"You!" she said, looking fiercely at Victoria, still not believing that this was her child. "You're the little street walker that Willie's telling everyone is my daughter, aren't you?"

Stunned and offended, Vickie took a deep breath and as she did, she put her nail file back into her purse and set it to the side. Victoria was not easily provoked. Normally, it took more than a verbal insult to rile her. I've learned a great deal about her in such a short amount of time, and one of the things I've discovered is that it takes a lot to rattle her cage. She's endured name calling many times before, being in the line of work she's in, but something about hearing those words coming from Mary struck a nerve. She could sit still no longer.

"What did you just say to me?"

"I want to know what scam you and Willie are trying to run on me and Thurston?"

Everyone began looking around, trying to figure out who

Mary was talking about. She had initially come across very lucid and sound in trying to get to the nature of Vickie's presence. But who was Thurston?

"Speak up, now. I want to know," she continued. "The Howells have worked too hard for our money, and we are not about to let no fake deacon, bootleg preacher, no prostitute, no Skipper, no Professor, Ginger, or MaryAnn take our money! Do you hear me, missy?"

In one long declaration, she'd moved from the Madison High-rise Apartments and Condominiums, to a deserted island. Weldon scratched his head and said, "How in God's name did we end up on *Gilligan's Island?*"

Betty saw that Victoria was moving slowly toward Mary with a cross look on her face. Normally, my sister would have pulled out some money and started betting on who would win the fight, but instead she tapped Vickie on the shoulder to get her attention. When Vickie turned around, Betty went there.

"I don't know if you're a sidewalk tramp or not, but you, your pimp," she said, pointing at Weldon, "and your madam," she pointed at Mary, "better get y'all's little fast, hot tails out of my house right now!"

"Your house?" Victoria shot back at Betty. "Lady, this is not your house! Who are you, anyway? How are you—"

"Street hussy," Mary interrupted, "don't turn your back on me and go talking to that old, senile woman over there! I'm talking to you, and you better give me your undivided attention!"

Now Weldon ought to have known that it's absurd trying to stop a woman from getting her point across, especially when she's dead set on reading another sister the Riot Act. It's hard enough attempting to calm down one woman, but in this case, there were three. That clown, however, still gave it his best shot and tried to put out the multiple fires that were beginning to rage. He, in his indescribably stupid wisdom, set out to divert their attention from snapping on one another. I guess he thought he would help them find common ground and lead them toward a civilized discussion. Yeah right.

"Hello," he said to Betty in his Sunday morning preacher tone. "So, you must be the lovely lady Tina was telling me about earlier. It's a pleasure to meet you, even under these difficult circumstances. My name is Pastor Charles David Wel—"

"Old?" Betty screamed at Mary, not paying any attention to Weldon. "Well, I ain't too old to pull all them gray hairs out your nose and stick my foot so far up in your ..."

I knew it wasn't going to work. I knew it. Not only did they cut him off every time he tried to chime in, but they cut each other off as well. These were three black women, who were all now standing in the middle of my living room, shaking their necks and pointing their fingers at each other. Civility is certainly achievable when all parties respectfully agree to disagree and when name-calling is prohibited as part of the rules of engagement. Well, somebody must have forgotten to pass out the card with the rules on them, or if they did, these sisters decided to simply throw them in the trash.

"You'd better watch how you're talking to me, crazy lady!" Vickie yelled at Mary. "You might have those folk at the church afraid of you, but I don't allow anyone to talk to me like I'm some—"

"Hooker!" Betty blasted away at Vickie. "What do you mean this is not my house? I'm the queen in this here castle and what I don't understand is how, while I was on my throne, getting extra beautified and everything, y'all three stooges broke up into my place?"

Isn't it phenomenal how people can come into your world,

walk straight up into your domain, and act like ownership's been transferred? Now, I care about everybody that was in my place this morning, well except for you know who. On a normal day, once I've had plenty of rest, a hot meal, a long shower, and a top shelf Long Island, I'd be more than happy to play host to almost anybody. I might be a little coarse around the edges from time to time, but I'm really a very nice guy once you get to know me. I do, however, develop a rash all up my backside when people attempt to run me or my stuff. While I was down the block a bit getting some groceries and things, there were four folk going at it, and I believe Mary was the chief instigator.

"Preacher," she said to Weldon while looking abhorrently at Victoria. "Is this yet another one of your little floozies? We down there last night at the jail, fighting tooth and nail to get you out, and here I find you the next day consorting with this Jezebel, pretending to be my daughter!"

"Look now," Vickie replied, "you've got one more time to call me out of my name and I'm going to jail!"

"Victoria," Weldon interrupted, "now that's no way to talk to your elders."

Vickie knew he was right, but it was too late to try and be respectful, especially to these two. "Pastor, I didn't come over here to be insulted by two senior citizens, who need to be up in somebody's nursing home, drinking Ensure and sucking down some bowls of JELLO!"

I know it was loud in there and it was only a matter of time before one of my neighbors called the police. They told me that no more than thirty seconds after Vickie had suggested their age appropriate beverages, somebody was banging on the door. Sweet Jesus, I knew my home would never be the same. Who was trying to get into my place now?

Chapter 9: Willie's ENCOUNTER

"You have to take risks. We will only understand the miracle of life fully when we allow the unexpected to happen."
~Paula Coelho

No matter how many times I've walked into this store, it is always busy. Samboes wasn't anything like a Super Walmart or even a basic K-mart, for that matter. It didn't have the traditional selection of food choices like a Kroger or even a Safeway, but it was a little larger than your average mom-and-pop grocery store. It's one of the longest standing African American businesses in the neighborhood that's still owned and operated by the family who had launched it nearly eighty years ago. There are many reasons for its survivability through various wars, the Civil Rights Movement, unscrupulous land developers, and money-grubbing politicians, who've tried everything to obliterate it. It's still standing because the cantankerous spirit of Pop Donald P. Samboes, the founder and mastermind of this single establishment, is alive and well in the heart of his grandson Cordell.

Everyone says that Cordell not only looks like his grandfather, but he acts like him too. No matter who you are, if he's working the register or happens to see you when you walk in, you are greeted by a blunt and straight forward, "Good morning. Now, what the f--- do you want today?" There's no need to take offense because it's not meant to be offensive. The Samboes have always been cursers and they don't hardly say anything without using the f-word as a part of normal conversation. Pop Samboes cussed all the time, especially on poker night in the basement every Thursday and Sunday evening. Grandma

Samboes cussed while shucking corn and baking fresh bread because it soothed her thoughts and helped her concentrate. All of their fourteen children cussed like sailors in school, and it was so normal that the teachers finally stopped reprimanding them and sending them to detention. The legacy continues and is alive and well in Cordell, who is one of the fifty-three grand-children and the current store manager.

At one point, all of the family has worked at the store in one capacity or another. Just like some fathers demand their children grow up and attend church every Sunday, Pop required that all members of his household put in their time working for the family business and provide jobs for the community he loved. He believed in helping people, especially those in dire straits, but you had to earn it. He wasn't giving anything away. For example, if you were a woman whose husband had left you to raise four children on your own, Pop would give you a job in the store, but he'd put a time limit on it. You stayed there no more than three years, and in those years, he made you save as much money as you possibly could. He taught them that his store was there to provide a hand up and a way out. It was never meant for you to make it a career. He would teach you everything about how to create and run your own business and push you to become a success on your own. Pop felt that blacks needed to have their own and stop depending on the white man to provide for them and give them scraps from the master's table.

I walked on into the store, fully expecting the standard greeting, but to my surprise, it did not come. I found out later that Cordell was in the back, dealing with two of the employees who had gotten into a fight a few minutes before I had arrived. He wasn't out front greeting those of us who walked in, but we all clearly heard him utilizing, in great form, the curse word vocabulary that had been so thoroughly engrained into him by a loving, but stern grandfather. The store was filled with patrons, as it always seemed to be, and in any other public setting, you might expect a group hearing this type of commotion to be stunned and shocked by what they've heard. You might expect that in a normal establishment, but this was far from what you would call normal. Nowhere else would you find such a diverse group of people assisting each other in accomplishing their goals like you did in Samboes. This was a twenty-four-hour, seven-days-a-week operation and it ran smoother than even the local sheriff's department or the county courthouse. Everyone was very respectful of the other's space and time and it was not strange at all to see the biggest gangbanger in the hood working with the police deputy chief to help an elderly lady shop for her weekly groceries.

Another reason why this corner store was so popular was the wide variety of soul food you could get here around the clock. For example: Down the meat aisle, there was an assortment of fatback, ham hocks and hog jowls. Down the next aisle, you'd find the black-eyed peas, collard greens, and mustard greens. When you walk toward the seasoning and condiment section, you find the onions, garlic, and vinegar. I could go on and on, but I'm sure you get the point.

I know that everybody cooks and eats in every culture and in every country, but I completely feel like we do it better than anyone else. It's just something our people seem to be able to do, regardless of our age or stage in life. My cousin Elroy has got to be New Jersey's biggest drunk, but his barbecue ribs, chicken, and beef tips will make you slap the taste out of somebody's mouth. There's a hooker who lives in apartment 5-B in my building. Her breath stinks so bad that it can stop a freight train and she's got more hair up under her armpits than Don King has on his head. Oh, but good God Almighty, that sister can *do* the doggone thing when it comes to baking a sweet potato pie. Even my sister Betty-Jean, who gets on my last nerve, will make you hurt yourself when it comes to them chitlins and hog jowls. I don't know what she does to make them taste the way they do. I mean they melt in your mouth and you eat until your gut's about to explode.

I went down to the store this morning to get some lunch-meat, crackers, fruit, aspirin and a few other things. This was not my regular shopping day; besides, I had walked there and didn't want to have a lot of heavy bags to carry back home. More than anything, I had to get away from Fred and Aunt Esther and I was not going to be home when Mary the Terror came by. My plans were to take my time and walk up and down every aisle as slowly and calmly as I could. I was not in a hurry to go anywhere. Besides, Mell's Package Store was right next door and I was certain they had plenty of what I needed. My plan was to stop by there and pick up some supplies before making my way back home. I needed peace at that moment, and I felt like this would be the place where that goal would be achieved. Until I heard ...

"Umph, umph, umph. I just knew your fat head should have still been behind some bars this morning."

When I heard the voice that was coming from behind me, there was no need to turn around and see who it was. I recognized it immediately and dropped my head in disbelief. I closed my eyes, took a deep breath, bit down on my bottom lip, and wondered what I had done to invite this intrusion into my space of tranquility. I replayed the last twenty-four hours of my life and immediately asked God to help make sense of it all.

I had started out in church and led devotion, like I always do. I endured the repetitive and boring prayer of Deacon Winderson, who normally puts me to sleep with his pitiful attempt at intercession. After that, I sat through an A, B, and C selection from the choir and did all I could not to throw up when Q.T. shook his skinny butt as he directed those tone deaf singers. Weldon took forever to come out of his office and God only knows what—or who—he was doing back there. Mother Johnson woke up after a good thirty-minute nap and decided to break out in one of her awful hymns that don't nobody know the words to but her. I had taken all I could, and I might be wrong, but I had to get out of there. I respectfully extended my pointer finger up, lowered my head, waited until she finished her second song, and then tiptoed myself right on out the side door. Low and behold, there I was a few hours later, spending the evening in jail with Weldon.

It seemed like everything and everybody had done whatever they could to get on my nerves. The guards had stuck me in the lower level of the jail, knowing good and well that I prefer to be on the main floor. That dude Anthony kept singing and prophe-lying almost the entire time we were down there, trying to make me believe that he knew everything about me. The vent that came into my cell allowed me to hear the noise and foolish talking that some of the church members were doing up in the lobby above me. When they brought Weldon's trifling behind inside, they had the audacity to lock him up in the cell next to mine, and all he did was whimper and whine all night long. The worst part, however, is when that big-butt, ghetto fabulous, loud-talking woman snuck in there and did her best to flirt with Weldon. She and I had gotten into some mudslinging and started badmouthing each other for a good while last night.

133

She had finally left and I thought I'd seen the last of her. Who would have known that this morning, Wanda had decided to shop in the same store as me.

"What are you doing here?" I said, not even turning around to look at her to acknowledge her presence.

"I'm in here to go skinny dipping, stupid. What do you think I'm doing in here?"

"Stupid?" I had to turn around now and address this chick face-to-face. I can be a lot of things for a lot of people, depending on what they need me to be, but I cannot be anybody's stupid. "You may want to tone that down, young lady, and learn to respect your elders."

"So now that you're somewhat sober, you want to talk about respect? The last I checked, respect goes both ways, doesn't it?"

"What are you talking about?"

"Oh, so now you got amnesia, huh?"

"I haven't said anything disrespectful to you."

"Old man, you didn't even know me last night. I wasn't in that place more than five minutes when you decided to run your mouth about me."

"What do you expect? I mean who sneaks into a jail to flirt with a preacher? It appears to me that you don't have respect for yourself."

"You don't know what I was doing and why I was down there to see the minister. You should have minded your own business, old man, and stayed out of mine."

"Girl, you don't have no business I want."

"So why were you eyeing me so hard and this business in the back of my jeans if I don't have nothing you want."

"You trippin'."

"Ain't nobody trippin'. I know you want this right here. Like

I said, you're old, not dead. You want to crawl up all over this good candy, but you can forget that. You don't have enough money, and I don't do senior citizen discounts."

"Well, let me give you whatever money I do have, and see if I can pay you to get the hell up away from me. How about that?"

"You're a feisty little deacon, aren't you?"

"And?"

"So, do all of you deacons cuss and try to get in young women's pants?"

"What are you talking about?"

"You know good and well what I'm talking about."

"Ain't nobody trying to get in your pants! That's the *last* place I want to be."

"Whatever. Where's that fine preacher man of yours?"

"No, don't change the subject. I need for you to retract that statement you just made. I don't need anyone thinking that I'm trying to get with you."

"Old man, you not fooling anybody. When I walked up in that jail last night, you practically undressed me with your eyes. I saw you, but I decided not to pay you no attention."

"All you saw was an opportunity to get some money out of Weldon."

"That's right! When you need money, you go to the ones who got the money."

"What makes you think he's got money? We don't pay him a lot at the church."

"Don't try to lie to me. That man dresses fine, he drives fine, he is fine, and I know his bank account is real fine. All pastors got money."

"So you think a three-piece suit and a BMW means that you're rich? You don't have a clue."

"Well, baby, if he don't have a bunch of money, he definitely knows how to go get it."

"What are you talking about, girl?"

"I see that man stand up there and raise that offering. I'm sure it's no less than twenty-five thousand dropping in that collection plate."

"It's nowhere near twenty-five thousand dollars, and that's not his money, anyway; it's the church's."

"He's the pastor and that means he runs the church, and if he runs the church, then he runs the money."

"He don't run nothing over there! It's quite clear that you don't know how the Baptist church runs."

"I don't have to know how it runs. It's a business, like everything else. The pastor is the CEO and he controls the money."

"Oh, you're real ignorant, aren't you? Let me please finish my shopping and get up out of here before you make me cuss for real."

"I'm gonna let you go, Deacon, but let me ask you a question first."

"What?"

"How is it that you're a deacon and a drunk? Y'all don't have no rules up in the church?"

"Do I look drunk to you?"

"You may not be drunk now, but the way I heard it, you be tore up all the time."

"I don't have time to talk to you and you don't have a heaven or hell to put me in."

"So you saying I can't ask you how you're still allowed to be a leader in the church when everyone knows you're an alcoholic?"

I don't know if it was what she'd said, the way she'd said it, or if maybe this time, hearing it hit me harder than expected. I know why I started drinking; I mean that was easy to understand.

I saw things in the bush that no man should have to see. When you take a man's life, even in war, it never really leaves you. When you realize that the bullet you fired pushed a man's eye into the back of his head, that image lies deeply in your heart. Your adrenaline and fear take over and as you rush forward to finish him off, you see him lying there choking on his own blood. That does something to you. I know why I took that first drink, but I couldn't explain why, in thirty years, I haven't been able to stop.

There were times when I'd quit and thought I had it licked, but then something always happened. It was how I dealt with the pain. The day I thought I'd lost the first woman I fell in love with. The year I got married and then lost my car and my job. The day I learned my wife and daughter had been killed. The day my true pastor was murdered out there in front of the church. After you survive one devastating trial, you think that's it, but before you've fully recovered, another shows up. I know people say that's how life goes, but when does it stop going wrong? When do you get to a point that your down days are behind you and your better days arrive? When do you wake up from the weeping and walk into a day of unending joy? Does it really happen? Is it true that trouble won't last always? If I knew that there was nothing too hard for God, then why had I still been relying on the booze to mask my pain? She had hit a nerve.

"Willie? Willie? Where did you go? I asked you a question and I'm standing here waiting on an answer."

The sound of her voice interrupted my thoughts and brought me back to the reality of where I was. I'm sure it hadn't been more than a few seconds that I stood there in deep thought, but it was enough time to allow her to see the blank stare on my face. I closed my eyes for a brief moment in order to divorce myself from my thoughts. When I reopened them, to my surprise, this girl was standing before me, eating some Vienna sausages out of a can that she'd snuck and opened. I looked down at the floor to see that she'd spilled or poured the Vienna juice on the floor near the bottom edge of the store rack. I could not believe what she had done and she stood there looking at me like I had the problem. This meeting and this conversation needed to end now.

"Wanda, listen," I said. "I'm busy. I've got things to do, and I'm not getting into this with you today."

"Deacon, I don't care," she shot back. "'Cause please understand, I didn't come in here to talk to you anyway. Listen, you tell that fine preacher, when you see him again, that we've got some unfinished business to discuss. Now, move out the way, fool."

I stepped out of the way and almost slipped in the juice as she and her shopping cart nearly hit me. She walked past and headed down the aisle, mumbling or humming something under her breath. I couldn't understand it and really didn't care what it was anyway. Instinctively, I watched her go down the aisle and had to admit to myself that as ratchet and nasty as she was, she had a booty that, my Lord, spoke to my inner loins. It was big and juicy, and everybody who knows me knows that's how I like 'em. It sat up on some thick, hard, yummy thighs that made a brother's hair stand up. Well ... something stood up. Anyway, I've always been a butt and thigh man and even though I'd never admit it to her, she had wonderful junk in that trunk. If anyone were to ask me what I thought about her or if I'd ever get with her, I'd tell them they were damn crazy. That's what I'd say with my mouth, but with my mind, I'd wear that thing out!

I had to shake my head and regain my composure. I turned back around and proceeded to do what I went there to do. I was in the aisle with the saltine crackers, so I grabbed a box and headed up the aisle to locate the other items I needed. I got to the end of the aisle and turned left to head toward the pharmacy area, when I heard another voice call my name.

"Deacon Willie, what the f--- you doing up in here today?"

Yep, you already know who that was. It was Cordell, who had come out of his office, followed by two young men who were wiping tears from their eyes, hanging their heads down low, and carrying their jackets as they headed toward the exit.

I said, "Hey Cordell, how are you doing, son?"

"I'm all right, Mr. Willie. I just had to go in on some knuckleheads who thought this was the f'ing place to handle their dispute over some f'ing girl both of them were doing. They should have known they got the wrong one."

"Yeah, it looked like you read them pretty good back there."

"They're lucky I didn't go upside their heads. You know, if Pops were still alive, he most definitely would have slapped the f--- outta them."

"Oh, I have no doubt about that. Your grandfather was a good man, but didn't take mess from nobody."

"Yes, sir. You know it. So how you been, Mr. Willie? I heard you got into a little trouble with the law yesterday."

"Oh, you heard about that, huh?"

"Man, you know don't nothing happen out here in these streets that don't get around. Negroes gonna always put your business out there."

"Yeah, that's true. I spent a little time downtown last night, but it's all good. I'm out and everything's everything."

"I heard your preacher man was up in there too. Did you run into him?"

"Run into him? I did more than run into him. I had to sit up and listen to him whine and complain the whole time he was in there."

"Oh wow! Are you serious?"

"Yes, sir. They put him in the cell right next to mine. When I tell you he got on my nerves, it was ..."

Suddenly, Cordell tapped me twice on my chest as his eyes opened really wide. He was looking at something down the aisle that had quickly caught his attention. I turned to look in the same direction and discovered that his radar had zoned in on Wanda's butt. She was moving away from us, but I could see that she'd opened a bag of skins, placed it in the upper section of her cart, and was eating them while reaching for other items on the shelves.

"Man, I know you're a deacon and everything down at the church, and you can't be lusting and all about these ladies, but man, look at that girl's f'ing tail right there! Umph, now wouldn't you, no doubt, wanna jump all up into that?"

"Now Cordell, you must have lost your mind. There's no way in the world I'd have anything to do with that woman. She's nasty."

Don't judge me. I told you I'd never admit it out loud. Anyway, I waited for Cordell to finish oohing and awing about Wanda, and when she walked out of his line of sight, I brought him back so we could continue our conversation. "Are you finished, son?"

"Dawg, Mr. Willie, that thing just called out my name!"

"Listen, I'm telling you, you don't want to be bothered with that one there. All she cares about is how much money you make."

"Deac, if she let me hit that like I want to, I'll give old girl some money!"

"You give that girl some money, and she's gonna end up owning this whole store."

"Nah, I ain't gonna let her do all that, now. Ain't nobody 'bout to mess me up like that, Deac."

"Listen, she's gone now. Where's your aspirin? I've had a nagging headache for a minute and I gotta pick up something to get rid of this."

"I gotcha, Mr. Willie. Sorry about that. She threw me for a minute. The pain meds are right over there in aisle four. Help yourself. I've gotta get back to my office and get ready for a shipment coming in shortly. It was good seeing you. Have a good day."

We shook hands like the brothers do, and I headed toward aisle four. I got everything I needed and headed for the register. I grabbed some gum as the cashier scanned my few items, paid her, and walked out the store. I stepped out, turned to my left, and could see through the window that Mell's Package Store only had a few customers inside. So, I walked on in.

Chapter 10: Willie's FAMILY

"Happiness is having a large, loving, caring, close-knit family in another city." ~George Burns

BACK AT MY PLACE, THE SAGA CONTINUED AND THE DRAMA WAS in high gear. Vickie, Betty, and Mary were raising the roof, and without a doubt I knew it was going to get worse before it got better. You can't put three headstrong and inflexible women in the same room and think that whatever conflict exists can be calmly and quietly discussed in a rational and civil manner. Civility was a wrap the moment Mary had burst into the room. Betty and Vickie didn't even realize that the reason they were so comfortable slinging cheap shots at each other is because they've got the same blood running warmly through their veins. It was going down like a triple "Thrilla in Manila," but this time Muhammad Ali, Joe Frazier, *and* Mike Tyson were added to the mix. Now I don't know which one was which, but I'm sure each thought she was the heavy weight smack-talking champion of the world.

What's truly sad is I knew that Weldon didn't have a clue on how to handle these three strong black women this morning. He's used to dealing with weak, illiterate, submissive young girls, who think his voice sounds as sultry and seductive as Lou Rawls or Barry White. He's bragged about women fighting over him and hanging on his every word, like he was some freaking movie star or untouchable entertainer. That joker wasn't, and isn't, anything special. I don't get it. For the life of me, I can't understand what some of these silly women see in these preachers. Most of them don't do nothing but spin around and holler like they've rubbed Icy Hot on their groin instead of lotion. They get up there behind the book board, alter the tone of their voices, throw a little cadence into their speech patterns, and these simpletons in pantyhose lose their minds.

Now, that Pastor Bell ... that was a real preacher and a real pastor. When he preached, there was a lot of hollering, but it wasn't coming from him, it was coming from the congregation. He could get the hardest, coldest, unreachable brother in the sanctuary to a point where he would be just bawling like a baby. He would stand up there and explain the depth of Jesus's suffering so descriptively, until there was not a dry eye in the house. We'd all be on our knees repenting for what we'd done and said that week. Some preachers barely say three words, and they're off to the races, tuning and moaning like they've really said something deep. My pastor, Pastor Bell, however, was the definition of poise and power in the pulpit. He could take one small piece of one scripture and work that thing for over an hour. When other preachers would come over and hear him, they would say that nobody could exegete a text like Bell. They said he was masterful at hermeneutics and homiletics, or something like that. You know I don't much understand that preacher talk. One more thing they would say about him is that he really knew how to break down the etymology of a word. I miss that man. I wish he was back in my place, dealing with my sister and them instead of Weldon.

The whole time I was in the store, I had a funny feeling that something crazy was going down in my place. I had no way of being certain about that until I got back later and was brought up to speed about everything that had transpired. I told you that somebody was banging on the door and I figured it was the police, responding to complaints. Most of the time, the neighbors were used to hearing somebody fighting in the building or loud TVs and music playing at all hours of the night. If it wasn't a baby crying that woke you up from a good nap, it was a group of teenage boys banging on the walls, trying to keep rhythm while rapping about life in the ghetto. You got used to loud noises in my building, but the yelling, cursing, and fussing coming from my apartment was abnormal, and everybody knew it. Like I said, I thought it was the police, but I was wrong. It was Tina again.

"Hey, are you people crazy? I'm upstairs trying to watch *Good Times* but can't hear nothing 'cause of all the fussin' and cussin' going on in here!"

She had started yelling from outside the door, but by the time she'd informed the folk that they had interfered with her being able to watch James and Florida, she was already inside. Apparently, she'd come back down with the master key, and instead of waiting to see if someone was going to open the door, she proceeded to let herself in. She was still wearing the same outfit, but this time she was barefoot and there were cotton balls stuffed between each of her toes. She walked down the hallway toward the living room and was greeted right away by Betty, who saw her first.

"Oh look," Betty said with a look of disgust on her face, "the Loch Ness monster is back. Somebody call the circus and let 'em know one of their clowns done escaped."

Tina walked in on the heels of her hoofs, trying very hard not to smudge the fresh purple toenail polish adorning her unwashed, crusty, and ashy feet. Initially, her attention was on everybody and anybody who was responsible for the ruckus in the apartment directly below hers, but when Betty shot off at the mouth, she refocused her attention on her and her alone.

Maybe she figured that Betty wouldn't pick up right where she'd left off a little while ago. My sister may be old, but she's sharp as a tack and she reminded Tina that their argument had never ended due to the phone call I had received from Mary. This was an opportunity for the folly to resume. Only this time, there were more players in the room. Betty drew first blood, but I was told that Tina came right back, quick, fast, and in a hurry.

"Better yet," Tina replied, "y'all need to call the zoo and let them know that they are missing one of their hyenas."

Betty and Tina were going at it again, but Vickie's eyes were squarely concentrated on Mary. She could not believe that Mary had called her a floozy and a Jezebel and didn't even know her. Vickie works in a nightclub that's filled with men who become verbally abusive when they get drunk and want the dancers to do more than dance. In a matter of minutes, she can go from being called the most beautiful queen they've ever seen, to the biggest stuck up whore, who's too ugly to do anyway. She's become numb to name-calling, and not knowing the patrons makes it even easier to dismiss what they call her without a second thought. Today was different. This was different. Vickie had barely slept last night, playing over and over again in her mind what I'd said in that lobby. I hadn't told her yet about Mary because I wanted to get to know my daughter well before I hit her with the news about a mother who was lost in a world of delusion and fantasy. I didn't know how to tell her that I had recently found her mother myself and she didn't even remember what the two of us once had. It's so crazy that it's even hard for me to make sense of it sometimes.

"Where's my oil?" Mary said, interrupting the back and forth between Betty and Tina. "I needs to anoint every last one of you in here! I have been falsely accused of a crime of fornication and I needs to prove my innocence! That booger-shootin', bucktooth, shifty-eyed, bow-legged deacon has tarnished my good name, and it looks to me like all these devils in here need a greasing!"

Mary reached into her pocketbook and pulled out a bottle of Wesson Oil, unscrewed the top, poured some into her hand, and started flinging it all over the room. She started speaking in tongues and quoting scriptures from the Bible, while pleading the blood of Jesus against them. Everybody ducked and dodged, trying to avoid being doused with her version of healing ointment. Weldon, with his slow tail, attempted several times to remove the bottle from her hand, and finally did so, only seconds before she poured it all on his head.

"Lady!" Vickie shouted. "There's no way on God's green earth that you could be my mother! My mother died a long time ago! She's not some deranged, homeless woman, who has lost her freakin' mind! So if you came by here to get some answers, then like I told the preacher, I did too! Willie's got a lot of explaining to do!"

When Vickie said that, Betty-Jean immediately flipped around and grabbed her by the arm with a strange look on her face. She felt that Vickie was being very disrespectful by calling out my first name as if we were real close, or something. Her defenses went up right away. No matter what disagreements or disputes we may have as siblings, most of us will not idly stand by and let anyone talk about or disrespect a member of our family. Betty-Jean and I had our differences, as all brothers and sisters do, but she was always very protective about her little brother.

When I was in elementary school, my sister would routinely boss me around. She knew she could slap me around, but nobody else could. It was all right for her to call me four eyes when I got glasses, or metal mouth when I got braces, but nobody better say it in front of her. I got picked on sometimes and all I had to do was tell my big sister, and you best believe she went right to the source of the problem and handled her business. I'll never forget that day she walked right up into Leon's house and punched him in the nose while he sat at dinner with his family. That fool sister of mine fiercely looked at everyone sitting there, daring them to say a word. They knew their son was a bully and they knew that she was a brawler. Nobody said a word. She grabbed a piece of fried chicken off the table, took a swig of somebody's Kool Aid, and walked out the door like nothing happened. That's my sister, and it doesn't matter who you are. Like I said, she was very protective when it came to me, but there was a good reason.

I didn't learn until I was grown and in the military that Betty had it harder than I ever did growing up. Her father was a sick, decadent man, who started touching her inappropriately when she was only four years old. I could never understand how a man, any man, could damage a little child in that way. It would start with him coming into the room to check on her and make her feel safe and shielded from the Boogyman she thought lived in the closet. He knew she was afraid of the dark, especially during a rainstorm, and this was his way of pretending to be her protector and comforter. It was harmless, initially, and nobody would suspect anything otherwise. He would sit up in the bed and hold her while reading one of her favorite short stories. If that didn't completely put her to sleep, then he'd sing a lullaby, which seemed to always do the trick. That's how it began, but it didn't stay that way for long.

Soon, his sitting in the bed turned into lying beside her all night long. He would hold her tightly and kiss her gently on the top of her head. He told her that nobody could ever love her as much and as specially as her father could and that what they shared would always be their secret. This demon told her that a father and daughter could not be as close as they needed to be if their bodies were separated by t-shirts, pajama bottoms, and underwear. He would put some of her dolls and toys in the bed, and they would play together and make up adventures that she truly enjoyed. Under the covers, he showed her his, as he called it, special toy that stayed with him all the time. If she was a good little girl, then he would let her play with it.

She was so young and so desperate to please her father any way she could. She had no idea that what he'd coaxed her into doing was perverted. All of this was a game and she thought all kids did this with their fathers. The reason why Mama couldn't know about their secret adventures and fun never even came up. Sometimes, the games made Betty laugh out loud, but then there were times when it was painful. When it hurt, she'd cry out, but her daddy would always tell her that it wouldn't hurt forever and he would make the pain go away. This filthy dog would have her stretched out beside him in her bed. He was completely naked, and she was completely trusting. I know it went on for years before she discovered what this really was.

She never would tell me any more than that, but I knew the rest. I think around the time I started preschool, it had stopped. She found the strength to put a stop to it. She was fourteen then and big for her age. I heard that it came to a point where she decided to try to kill him, since he had been killing her for years. I don't remember all the details, but I do know that she'd hit him with something one night so hard that he spent more than a month in the hospital. They sent her off to juvenile for six months. Don't even ask me why. All I know is that it never happened again. Nobody ever messed with Betty-Jean again.

"Willie?" she said, still gripping Vickie's forearm. "Young lady, that's Mr. Lester to you!"

Vickie snatched her arm back and raised herself like she wanted to swing on Betty, but thanks be to God she chose another route, because that would not have been a wise move. Vickie is truly a good girl and she has the most adorable brown eyes that a father's ever seen. She wasn't raised in a family environment where fighting and bickering were the typical ways to resolve issues. Her adopted parents may not have gone to church on a regular basis, but they were well respected in the community. They were educators and community activists, who volunteered at homeless shelters and gave generously to children's hospitals. They invested their earnings wisely and vacationed as a family out of the country at least every other year. They spent every holiday together as a family and sat at the dinner table to eat every night without fail. This was the black version of *Leave It to Beaver* and everyone viewed them as the ideal family.

Vickie led, what many would call, the perfect life until that day she found out that her life was a lie. Not a lie in the sense that she wasn't genuinely loved, but a lie because the man and woman she'd always known as Mom and Dad, were not her real parents. She knew of a few other kids in school who were adopted or grew up in foster homes. She saw how cruel other children could be toward them and how alone and abandoned they felt at times. She couldn't imagine what it must have felt like, knowing that you were given away and left on a doorstep like a wrapped up newspaper. She had bragged about the health and wholeness of her family and was honored to be so revered in the neighborhood. That day, however, when she learned the truth, it did something to her. It created a deep wound in her heart, and it was only compounded by the revelation that her parents never bothered to share. How did a girl who came up on the right side of the tracks end up making a living by stripping in gentlemen's clubs?

I don't know the depth of her pain in full, but I do understand the jolt you feel when the foundation you've always stood on has been ripped from underneath you. I know what it is to put so much confidence in what others have told you, only to find out that they've been misleading you all along. True friends are hard to find and sometimes it takes years to discover that someone you thought was trustworthy may actually be your undercover enemy. You can handle it when a friend betrays you, but it's not supposed to be that way with family. Family is supposed to hold you up when others let you down. Family is supposed to push you forward when others hold you back. Family is supposed to believe in your dream, even when others consider it a nightmare. Family is all we have, or what we're supposed to have. Truthfully, there are times when family is the biggest challenge in your life. My Vickie was now meeting her real family.

Weldon saw that things were escalating to a level beyond staunch words and cut-throat insults. He knew he'd better try again to be the peacemaker and get these, now, four women to calm down and stop all the fighting and name-calling. Everybody was confused and I'm sure they were all looking for me, but I was, at that time, getting my stuff and leaving Mell's Package Store after surveying the various new products this fine establishment had received. I was strutting along the sidewalk, making my way back, while some family and folk were in my domain, traumatizing the whole building.

"If you people would stop yelling at one another long enough for us to have an intelligent conversation, we could get this all worked out!" the good preacher yelled.

Maybe that worked with women who respected his title or those who were admirers of his education, or even those who had the pleasure of his company away from church. Maybe yelling and pointing his finger at those types of ladies had worked for him in the past, but it did not work for him this morning. It's bad enough to raise your voice at a group of black women who are already perturbed and tired of being slandered, but what man in his right mind doesn't know that one of the worst things you could ever do is put your finger in a sister's face?

"Preacher," Mary said as she slapped his finger away like Sophia slapped the taste out of Harpo's girlfriend's mouth in Harpo's Juke Joint, "we are not at church and you are not moderating a meeting, so why don't you just sit your little self down or move out of my way so I can address the lies and vicious rumors this girl has been saying about me!"

"Now wait a minute, Sis Mary—" Weldon interjected.

"No, you wait a minute!" Mary screamed. "And boy, let me help you understand one thing. If you ever put your finger in my face again, you gonna lose that finger and at least three or four more in the process! Do you hear me?"

While Tina was upstairs watching her sitcom and getting a private pedicure form some idiot man, she was unable to clearly hear what everyone was fussing about below. She was not happy in the least bit that she had to ask her male friend to stop what he was doing so she could find out what was going on in my apartment. As much noise as I have to deal with flowing from her place most weekends, she ought never have an attitude or a problem with what was coming from my home this morning. I don't have a lot of company and I never throw parties. I don't have a bunch of guys over to watch the game or have members from the church here for meetings or socials. No one complains about the noise coming from my apartment because there's never any noise to complain about. She knew this was an odd day and was undone when she discovered what the uproar was all about.

"You mean to tell me you all are down here fighting and arguing over what Deacon Lester said last night at the jail house?" Tina said. "This is why my pampering session got put on hold? Are you kidding me?"

Betty was outraged. "Wait, wait, wait a minute! Jail? What do you mean my brother said something from the jail house last night?"

I wish I had made it back in time to stuff some tissue in Tina's grill. I swear she's always got that mouth open, saying things that don't need to be said. When I saw the church members in the lobby last night, I knew a bunch of them would be talking and gossiping about me. You know that's what we do better than anything else. It's sad to admit it, but I've been around long enough to know that to be true. It didn't matter though, because they operate in small circles, so what they said wouldn't go that far. But when I looked up and saw Tina, I knew my name and picture would be all over the city in less than twenty-four hours. We don't even watch the local news around here anymore, because nobody's coverage is more detailed and precise than Tina's.

"Your brother?" Vickie asked of Betty. "Mr. Lester is your brother?"

Mary wasted no time jumping back into the dialogue, and what she said next was vintage Mary. "I knew it! Lord Jesus, I just knew it! It's a generational curse! They all a bunch of liars, gamblers, crooks, and thieves! They sleep around, dance naked on tables, fight each other like gangsters, and cuss at least five days a week! It's all in the family, Jesus! And Lord, they trying to say that I'm a part of this family, but I know that's a lie! I'm too respectable to be related to these heathens, Father God!"

There is no dealing with a woman who can't figure out if she's here or gone from one minute to the next. In the short time that Mary's been back, I've never seen her wearing the same two shoes on her feet. On her right foot, she may have on a black Nike sneaker, and on her left foot may be a pink pump that she found in the dumpster behind the Goodwill. She may show up to church in a jogging suit that went out of style back in the 70s, or she may walk up in there wearing a wedding gown. You never know. She was off her rocker this morning, but Betty didn't care at all about that. She didn't allow anybody to talk about her family.

"Where's my shotgun?" my sister raged. "I promise, I've had it with this big, crazy one over here! What she needs is a good buckshot up in her fat behind!"

"Wait!" Tina chimed in. "Don't hit her till I get my phone out. I need to make sure this gets on Facebook and YouTube. Y'all down here are so ratchet and you already know I love it. Okay, I got my phone now; so you can proceed with the beat down."

"Tina," Weldon fussed back, "put that phone away, girl, and stop acting crazy! Everybody, sit down so we can get to the bottom of this!"

"Yes, stripper!" Betty-Jean said to Vickie. "Willie is my baby brother, young lady; but why is that a concern of yours?"

Betty was the only one in the room who hadn't heard what I'd said last night and I was planning to tell her upon my arrival back home, but it got out before I made it back. Vickie had no reason to hold back the truth.

"Why am I concerned, you ask? Because Willie is my father."

The two of them stood there, looking at each other in a state of shock and wonderment at how they could possibly be related. Not like second or third cousins or connected because somebody had married somebody else. No, if what was being disclosed was true, they were auntie and niece. My family was finally discovering the truth, and wouldn't you know it … that was also when I walked back into my door.

"Betty-Jean, you still here?" I asked. I walked in, turned and closed the door behind me, turned back around, and looked up. There were five people looking hard at me like they all wanted my head on a platter. Yep, I was back home.

Chapter 11: Willie's HEART

"One ought to hold on to one's heart; for if one lets it go, one soon loses control of the head too." ~Friedrich Nietzsche

SOMEBODY ONCE SAID THERE'S NO PLACE LIKE HOME, BUT APPARENTLY, whoever said that had no idea of what my home looked like when I got back from the store. I had three bags in my hand, my jacket still on my shoulders, and my hat comfortably atop my head. I was reminiscing about the fun I had coming back through the neighborhood, this time with no interruptions or flying chew from an old lady's mouth. The peace I had experienced outside was nowhere to be found now that I was back inside. I thought for a second that maybe I should turn around and go right back out the same way I'd come. Something told me when I was riding up in the elevator that trouble was awaiting. At the time, I had no idea that three more people were in my living room, and the two that were there when I had left had no desire to leave. It was never clearer than at that moment why I had picked up the gallon-sized jug of Hennessy from Mell's this time, but I was absolutely glad that I had.

I remembered reading in the Bible (or somebody told me it was there somewhere) that God won't put more on you than you can bear. They said that He wouldn't allow you to go through something without giving you the strength to bear it. A lot of people have told me through the years that you're not supposed to question God. I get that, and for the most part, I've done good about that, but there have been times when I couldn't hold my peace. There were questions that I needed answers to, and He was the only one who had them. I wanted to know why He thought I had the strength to handle things that I didn't agree should happen in the first place. Like why did He let that punk of a man take my mother's life, just when she'd finally gotten up the courage to leave his sorry tail? I wanted to know what sense it made to stand there and allow my best friend to be blown to bits when the bomb was meant for me instead. How could a God, who is supposed to love and protect me, allow a teacher to grope my genitals and screw up my head? Most of all, why did He not protect my wife and daughter when that idiot, high on heroine, ran them down like dogs and left them to bleed out in the middle of the street? I was angry with God for a long time and for a lot of reasons. I was angry, but no matter how mad I became, I still went to church. Now what sense does that make?

There were Sundays, I admit, when I stayed home, trying to prove to God that I didn't need Him. I figured that since He wasn't looking out for me and mine, I wouldn't be studdin' anything He was trying to say to me. I would wake up, refuse to shower, and not even attempt to change out of my pajamas. I'd walk around, trying my best not to care about what might be happening down at the church in my absence. I'd drink whatever liquor I had in the house until I could hardly stand on my own two feet. I didn't want to have any connection in my heart about whether the service was anointed or if the atmosphere was charged. I was upset because He had done nothing to prevent all these bad things from happening to me, so I did whatever I could to show him that I didn't give a damn either. I stayed home and pouted like a big baby. I told myself that I was never going back. Yeah right. ... It never lasted more than a week. The next Sunday I was right back up in His house, crying and repenting for acting like a complete fool.

Giving your heart to God is more than you saying that He's your Lord and Savior. It's more than throwing up your hands during praise and worship or dancing in rhythm with the drummer and bass player. A lot of people say they are Christians, but what they really mean is that they are members of a church. They are under the impression that commitment to His Kingdom is based upon what ministry they've joined. To them, it's about singing in the choir or teaching a Sunday school class. It's about working with the media team or playing the organ. Church people will shout till their wigs fall off on Sunday morning, but will cuss, fight, and dog each other out every other day of the week. I know about church folk because I'm still one myself. I know right from wrong and I know that I should live better than I do.

I can hear my granny's scolding, telling me that if I don't obey her, I'm going to end up in hell. She was fire baptized and Holy Ghost filled to the utmost. Serving the Lord for her was not simply a Sunday morning thing; it was a way of life. She lived it seven days a week and pushed me and all my cousins to do the same. When anyone came to Granny's house, they received a lesson about Jesus before the sun went down. If you spent the night over there on Saturday, you best believe you were going to be in church Sunday morning, no matter how old you were. I can still see her down on her knees beside the bed, praying and asking the Lord to save my soul. Even after I got grown and moved away, I could feel her prayers still appealing my case. I know He's done more for me than Satan has done against me, and honestly I can't even tell you why I haven't gone ahead and given up all these things I do.

These were the thoughts going through my mind until they were rudely interrupted by the sound of Mary's voice. "There he is! There that man is! Y'all, let me go, 'cause I'm gonna get that one right there! Let me go! That's the man that says he and I have a baby!"

That's when I looked up and saw that Weldon was sweating and struggling, trying his best to keep my girl from running up on me. I looked over there and had to laugh a little bit because she was swinging him around like a paper doll. He was behind her with both arms wrapped around her waist, but she pulled him until he could barely keep from sliding. She had fire in her eyes and her fists were clinched tightly, as if she'd heard the bell ring for round one. I remembered how upset she was on the phone, but I had hoped that by the time she got here, she would have calmed down a little bit. I thought maybe the distance she had to come would have given her time to consider that I was not out to hurt or embarrass her. I was wrong. She was adamant about getting to the bottom of what she felt was the biggest lie anyone had ever told on her.

Women may forget a lot of things because some things are honestly not worth remembering. They will forget the name of the man who had wasted their time by taking them to a cheap restaurant and then asking them to split the bill fifty-fifty. They'll quickly forget the dumb line that some brother had fed them at the club while trying to convince them to let him get into their pants. They may even forget a girlfriend's name in high school, who had spent more time trying to compete with them than trying to defend them. They will forget some things, no doubt, but what woman have you ever heard about forgetting that she gave birth to a child?

"Willie," Betty-Jean cut in, "I know times are hard and all, but is it this bad? I mean, little brother, the best you could do was get with some old, nasty, back-alley, homeless, overweight chick? Boy, you should have never moved down here if this was what you had to choose from."

I swear you could always count on my sister to exacerbate a situation to a level it did not need to reach. I think she loved to stir up stuff, and no matter what day of the week it was, it was always a good time to try and create an altercation. She knew good and well that everyone was already dealing with their own frustrations about this issue in one way or the other, and instead of assisting the preacher man in calming the room, she decided to charge it. I think Betty vaguely remembered me talking about a woman I'd met when I first visited this city a long time ago, but she couldn't believe that Mary was that woman. She didn't want to think that her brother would drop to the level of being involved with someone who was mentally confused and physically challenged. What she didn't understand is that thirty years ago, Mary was one of the most beautiful women I'd ever seen. She was as classy as she was lovely. Nothing like these women around here, and certainly nothing like Tina, who had to jump up and get her two cents in.

"Willie, what kind of foolishness is this? You know I don't have no barnyard brawls in my building! I run a respectable place and I told you, I ain't having no foolishness in here today or any other day! Do you hear me?"

Everybody was yelling and nobody was giving me time to say anything. It was a free-for-all in here and whatever came up, came out. The gloves were off and the battle was on.

Even my Vickie was visibly upset to a point that I've never seen. "Daddy, what is this? I need for you to talk to me and tell me what's going on here!"

She was almost in tears, and for the first time since my wife and daughter passed away, I was about to break down as well. Something happened to me when I lost them. I vowed to never love or even care again to the degree that my heart would hurt again. When they were taken from me, I cried off and on for more than two years. Losing a wife and daughter at the same time throws you into a dark hole that's beyond anyone's reach. I had no more tears left for anyone and I refused to get close enough to a soul to develop emotions. I didn't hang out with people from the church. I didn't join any community organizations or attend any company parties. I didn't email much and I certainly didn't have a Facebook page. I drank more than I should have and I went to church out of habit and a promise I'd made to Pastor Bell. My world had enough in it with me and me alone. I wasn't looking for anybody and nobody, to the best of my knowledge, was looking for me. I had convinced myself that I didn't need anyone. My life was simple, quiet, and stress free. I didn't allow anyone to get close enough to affect my heart; that is until I met my Vickie.

I looked at her and saw how water began to form in the corners of her eyes. Her left leg was shaking a little bit and she was biting down on her bottom lip, trying to prevent anyone from noticing the anguish in her heart. She had picked her pocketbook back up off the floor and placed it on her left shoulder. With her right hand, she reached inside and pulled out her cell phone. I thought at first that she was about to call someone, but then I quickly realized that she was pulling up a photo to show me. She came close and turned the screen so I could plainly see who it was. It was a picture of her and me that was taken a little while ago at the park. We'd met there one afternoon and had the best time feeding the ducks and watching the people walk by. We ate hotdogs and cotton candy as we sat on the bench beside the little lake. It felt like the sun was shining brighter than ever before, and I remember not wanting that day to end. The smile she wore in that picture was not visible this morning in my apartment. I had to change that. It was time to connect all the missing pieces of this puzzle.

"Vickie, I see you've met your aunt and your mother. Sit down, baby. We have a lot to talk about."

I asked everyone to stop fussing and give me a minute to go into the kitchen and set these groceries down. They'd come at me so fast that I didn't even have an opportunity to free my hands. My head was still throbbing and I needed the Tylenol I had bought. I also needed a drink, a strong drink. I got ready to open my jug of Hennessy, but then strangely decided against it. I was so used to handling tough times in the same manner. My method of coping and healing was to completely pour myself into a bottle. Whatever crisis stood before me or whatever challenge I faced, it was easier to let the liquor take me to a place where I didn't have to care about my actions or what I said. It was easier to blame it, like Jamie said, on the alcohol. Everybody called me an old drunk and I didn't care because it was easier to walk away from life's problems than to stand sober and confront them.

I stood there for a minute, thinking back to the days when my life was different. Thinking back to a time before life's trials began mounting on me over and over again. I was promoted to sergeant in Uncle Sam's Marine Corp and my men respected me and followed me without question. They would do whatever I asked without hesitation because they trusted me with their lives. They watched me be the first to go into the hot zones and the last to leave the field of battle. Sobriety back then was a must and my high came from the numerous combats we won together as warriors. We left no man behind and we fought side by side until the threat was eliminated and the enemy destroyed. I was a man of honor and admired by my peers, subordinates, and superiors alike.

I thought about all of that as I stood, holding a bottle of death that had become my crutch. I had gone from being a distinguished man of valor to a despicable man of shame. I'd lost so much and ruined so much, but today I had been given a chance to make a change. I had a chance to do better. A chance to be better. God was giving me a chance and I was not about to mess this one up. I put that brand new jug in the trash and walked back into the living room, where everyone was sitting and waiting.

"First of all," I started, "I know my revelation last night was a shock to everyone and honestly, I don't know why I chose that moment to say what I said."

Before I could get the next word out, Mary jumped up from the couch and went ham on me. I thought by seeing the conciliatory look on my face and the calm in which I tried to import into the room, she would quietly sit there like everyone else and allow me to speak. She was moving her head back and forth, breathing hard, pointing her finger in the air, and showering me with spittle that came flying out of her mouth with each derogatory word. I guess she wasn't trying to hear no explanation at that moment. She didn't come for explanations; she came for answers. She came to jack me up and make me take back what I'd vocalized in the precinct last night. I may not have been able to clearly explain why I'd said what I'd said last night, but she had an answer.

"'Cause you a no-good, pickled-feet, bucktooth, lizard-lip, bad-breath, flat-butt, chicken-hearted, scandalous, old *liar!* That's *why* you said what you said last night, fool!"

"Mary, would you *please* shut up and sit down!" Now, those words came from Weldon and I must admit that I was floored when old boy jumped up and went off on Sis. Mary Ethel Maye. Finally, he realized that you can't talk sensibly to women who are unreasonable. That "Can we all just get along" spirit, may work in the upper scale communities and neighborhoods he's used to visiting, but not here. He's never, in my observation, been a man who handled confrontation well. I guess they taught him in seminary school to resolve discord with dialogue and discussion. Guys like him spend their days reading literature to enhance their oratory skills and debating techniques. He told me one time that preachers are taught to argue the text and challenge the listener to see the Lord in the full depth of His splendor. I don't know what the devil that means, but I guess it's what they learn to help them preach better on Sunday mornings.

Placid and composed communication is good and I'm sure it works in situations where the opposing party is equally motivated to resolve the conflict amicably. But most of the time, that don't work in the hood. Fancy words and respectful exchanges won't get you too far around here. Some folk don't understand nothing but a cuss or a slap, or both. Most of the people in my neighborhood didn't go to college. Shoot, most of them didn't even finish high school. They learned how to handle their business the old-fashioned way, and it was rare that an argument in my neighborhood ended without blows. Now, I'm not certain that a fistfight would have broken out at some point in my apartment this morning, but I didn't put it past any of these ladies. The conditions were truly ripe for it to go down like that. Mary was hot and when she jumped up on me, I knew that she was going to let me have it. So hear me when I tell you that we were all surprised when the hood came up out of Weldon.

"Now, we're up in this man's apartment, acting like barnyard animals! Y'all asking him questions but won't give him time to even answer! Sis Mary, I know you're my elder and I know you have some problems in your life right now, but you need to chill and let this man say what he needs to say!"

It worked for the moment. Mary looked stunned that Rev had spoken to her in that tone, but it did the trick, or so I thought. She may have calmed down for a minute, but my sister was still in stank mode.

"Willie, I comes back in here after getting extra fine, and all—you know how I do it—and there's a room full of crazies in *our* house, clowning and saying that this little *hussy* right here is supposed to be your daughter! Now, I been knowing you all my life, and the only child you had died a long time ago."

"Okay, I've had it!" Vickie interrupted. "I hope your denture cream is extra strength, old lady, 'cause I told you the next time you say something ugly about me, I was gonna slap all seven of the remaining teeth out of your mouth!"

"Well, bring it over here, Wonder Woman!" Betty shot back. "I'm itching to raise a knot on top of somebody's head in here today, and it might as well be yours!"

Tina grabbed the cell phone out of her back pocket and started dialing somebody's number. My sister and my daughter were literally about to go at it. Weldon stepped between them in time and tried again to keep them from snatching one another's weaves out of their heads.

"LaQuay," Tina said to her girlfriend on the phone, "this is better than Cookie and Anika on *Empire*, girl! It's about to be a cat fight in here … and it's an old, ugly woman verses a stripper, girl!"

"Tina!" Weldon yelled while trying to get Betty to stop kicking

JAMES E. CHANDLER, SR.

at Vickie. "Hang up that phone and quit stirring up mess! We don't need that in here!"

"That's right!" Mary stood up and said. "And you can't have none of my cornbread, either! That goes for you and all you other country bumpkins in here. You touch my cornbread, and it's gonna be consequences and repercussions!"

I looked over there at Mary, and I know my mouth was on the floor. I'm still trying to figure out how she thought, at that moment, she was Ray Gibson, talking to all the prisoners in the cafeteria in the movie *Life*. It was strange, but that's the world Mary lives in. There's no telling what was going on in her mind and what triggered her detachment from reality. Watching this was tough because I was the only person this morning who remembered what the real Mary was like. I was the only one who'd ever heard her speak and move people with the grace and ease of a master rhetorician. In her day, she didn't simply share the gospel; she brought it to life. When she would paint the picture of Jesus on the cross or Moses standing before the Red Sea, it was a work of art. She could describe those things in precise detail and everyone would be moved to tears before the end of her message.

She wasn't long-winded either. It didn't take her much time at all to put it down. My girl could do in twenty minutes what most male preachers couldn't do in hours. She was no nonsense when it came to talking about the God she loved and the Savior that had died for her sins. It seemed like she knew Him personally and they were the best of friends. I believe they were. I believe they still are. Her love for God was not based on what He'd given her or what He'd promised her, but it was based on who He was to her. She thanked Him for everything and she started off each day with no less than an hour of devotion and prayer. Her soul belonged to God and she gave Him full control of her life. She didn't have it easy growing up, but she was a survivor and knew where her help came from. That's why I came to love her like I did. That's why I still love her today.

Mary's dip into the world of a Hollywood movie tripped everybody out, but it also made them stop trying to fight one another. Vickie was hurting the most and she needed time for the two of us to discuss everything. "I really think that all of you should leave, so my father and I can talk in private. This is between him and me, and it doesn't concern any of you," she said.

"Young lady," Betty responded, "I told you my brother doesn't have any kids, and if he did, don't you think I would know about it? Maybe this schizophrenic over here has a point. Just what scam are you trying to pull on my brother?"

"Listen," Tina said in response to Betty's assertion, "you weren't there last night, so you don't really know what happened. Your brother said that she's his daughter. You can deny and dismiss it all you want, but it is what it is. Now, this is some of the best gossip I've heard in a while, so would you please turn your volume down so I don't miss anything?"

I don't even remember who was about to say something next or who may have been speaking, but enough was enough. It was time for Willie to have the floor. "Everybody, please sit down! I need to clear up some things. I need to talk to you from my heart."

Chapter 12: Willie's STORY

"There is no greater agony than bearing an untold story inside you." ~Maya Angelou

"Like I was saying before, I know my revelation last night was a shock to everyone, and honestly, I don't know why I said what I said last night."

I had barely begun where I'd ended before, when you know who jumped up to interrupt me again. She was about to go there, but the look on my face must have clearly said, "Oh, hell to the no," and Mary quickly sat right on back down.

This was going to be tough, and I knew it. I hadn't talked about this to anyone and disclosing my personal business was not something I was comfortable with at all. The last few months of my life had been a whirlwind of surprises and encounters, with resurrected feelings and emotions I'd buried in the past. How do you adjust and make sense of meeting a daughter you never knew you had? How do you come to grips with finding a love you thought was lost over three decades ago? So many years, I'd spent watching life circle me as if I were standing in the middle of a carousel, unable to get on. The ups and downs, the back and forth, the side to side seemed to never end and at the point when you give up on believing that life will get better, the unexpected arrives and swoops you off your feet. I stood there, looking at them looking at me and wondered if I could stay strong enough to tell my story. Seeing my Vickie, I knew I could.

"It's not that what I said last night wasn't true'; it's that I should have waited to say it when we were alone."

"Willie," Mary said, "why would you say that about me? Why would you tell these people that I have, that *we* have a child together? You don't understand what I've been through and what my life's been like out here on these streets. We don't even hardly know each other. I mean, your face looks familiar, but I don't know you, sir."

A pain shot across my chest when I heard and felt those words coming from her mouth. It was an unclouded moment. She was talking about all she'd been through the last few years and how much she's endured. She knew she'd been alone a long time but most of her memory was confined to the warm places where she could sleep and what restaurants dumped good food in the garbage at night. She didn't want to believe that it was even possible to have had a child out there and not know it. She looked at me with so much hurt and confusion.

"Mary, I know this is hard 'cause there are things you can't, or don't, want to remember. You see, you were driving back late one night from a revival meeting in a small town in South Florida somewhere. I heard you preached the house down and prayed for people well into the midnight hour. The pastor, who had invited you to preach, offered you a room in his and his wife's home. They tried to get you to stay overnight and then drive back home to Georgia in the morning. They tried, but you were adamant about getting home as soon as possible."

"This is not making any sense," she interrupted. "What are you talking about? I'm not a preacher man." She turned and looked at Weldon. "He's the preacher man. I don't know nobody in Florida! I've never even been to that place!"

"Please, Mary," Weldon said gently, grabbing her hand, trying to calm her down. "Listen, and let Deac continue. You came to get the truth. No matter how difficult it might be, you need to hear it."

"Mary, you were on your way back, and it was raining very bad that night. Every time I think about it, I wish to God that you would have only waited till morning or until the weather cleared up, but you didn't. An 18-wheeler came up beside you and, I don't know how, but they say he ran you off the road. You lost control and it was reported that your car had flipped several times on the road, until it ended up upside down in a ditch and against a tree. Apparently, the truck driver had no idea what he had done and he kept going down the interstate. He never slowed down or turned around to help you and see if you were all right. Oh God, Mary, that night changed our lives forever!"

I struggled to tell this story, and the look on her face was killing me. It was odd because I was informing her of a tragedy she had survived, but she couldn't remember any of it. She was trying so hard to conjure up a memory of that night or even that year, but no matter what I said, it was as if it had never happened. Weldon, Betty, Vickie, and Tina all sat still, almost transfixed, and listened to the event that changed so many lives.

I went on. "You weren't alone that night. You had your kids in the car with you—"

"Kids?" Betty said as she quickly slid to the front of her seat. "Y'all had a bunch of children, or something?"

"No, no Betty, not *our* kids! Mary's children." I bent down and sat on the coffee table in front of Mary and took her hand.

"You see, when I met you, Mary, you already had three small, precious babies. Your eldest one was only five years old. You told me that you got pregnant by your boyfriend in high school and both your parents forced you to get married. You said you tried to make the marriage work and even had two more children together, but this dude was no good. This dog of an ex-husband left you and the kids weeks after the youngest,

Elizabeth, was born. Mary, the kids were in the car with you that night."

Mary snatched her hand away from me and became very agitated and upset. "Why are you lying to me? What kind of man are you? Who would do this?"

"I'm not lying, Mary! I would never lie to you. This is why I didn't want to tell you earlier. I knew it was too much for you to take! I knew if you hadn't remembered anything about your life in all these years, it would be impossible for me to make you believe what I know to be true."

"So, Daddy," Vickie said, "what happened to the children? Are they alive somewhere?"

"No, baby, I'm sorry. They didn't make it. When they saw how badly the car was wrapped around that tree, the officers that had arrived on the scene assumed that everybody in the car had been killed instantly. That's what they thought, but Mary, you were still breathing. Your pulse was faint, but you were alive."

"Oh my God," Betty softly said, wiping a tear from her eye.

"The paramedics worked on you at the scene once the fire department cut you out of the car. You were rushed to the hospital. They thought they'd lost you, but somehow, someway, you kept fighting. They said you were in the hospital for a long time. You were in a coma for months, and somehow, by the grace of God, you just woke up one day. You opened your eyes. You had survived, but you couldn't remember anything."

Weldon had this puzzled look on his face, and I knew exactly what he was about to ask. He stood up again. "Hold on, Deac. This is getting weird. Okay, so where are you going with this? Where was her family? How does Vickie play into this story? You're not making any sense, man!"

"You think this is hard to hear and understand? Can you imagine how much more difficult it was for me! I lived it! I lived through it! You could never understand what this did to me. Let me finish, preacher! All of you are over here 'cause you wanted to know what happened, so allow me to finish."

I could not sit there on the table anymore. I had to get up and move around a little bit. Tina had gone into the kitchen and poured me a glass of water. I drank it down quickly, gave the glass back to her, and picked up where I'd left off. "Mary, what I don't understand is that when the police found you and pulled you from that wreck, you had no I.D. on you. You were driving a rental car that, as we found out later, one of your friends had gotten for you. The ambulance took you to the nearest hospital and started working on you right away. Your family didn't know what happened to you and it was a couple of weeks before they even found out where you were."

"Hold on, Willie," Tina cut in. "Where do you come in in all of this? You talking about her ex-husband, her children, her preaching revival in Florida, and all that, but I haven't heard much about you in this story."

"Okay, let me back up a little bit. As I said a minute ago, your children's father had left you after your youngest daughter was born. I didn't know you all then. It was about six months later when I came down here for the first time. I was on leave and always thought about visiting Atlanta, but up to that point, I hadn't. A buddy of mine grew up here and told me to check it out. He told me about Auburn Avenue Church and said that if I had a chance while in town, I should hear the preacher. So I did. I got up one Sunday morning and went to church. I'll never forget that day as long as I live because that's the day I first laid eyes on you. That's the day we met.

You were so young and gorgeous, and I remember saying to myself that I had never seen a woman as strikingly beautiful as you, Mary. I didn't waste any time. I started asking people in the church who you were and as soon as service was over, I introduced myself to you. You were a little leery about giving me your number, understandably so, but you did. We talked on the phone all week and made plans to see each other on Friday. That night was our first date. We went to dinner and had a ball. We talked and laughed the entire time. It was amazing how much we had in common and how well we'd hit it off in such a short amount of time. We spent almost the entire rest of my leave together, getting to know one another. I knew you already had three children by your ex-husband, but I didn't care at all about that. Every night, when I'd come back to my hotel, I would lie in my bed, thinking about what life would be like with the five of us as a family. I knew in my heart that one day I was going to ask you to marry me, and together we'd raise the kids to be good and loving children."

Mary looked at me with a long, deep stare. I could tell that part of her wanted so badly to remember the things I was telling her, but the other side wanted me to stop, because the truth was becoming too much to bear. After a moment, she cupped her head in the palms of her hands and began to tremble. She wasn't breaking down or anything, but I guess she was trying to hold on to reality. She was trying to stay connected to who she was at that moment and not allow her mind to venture off to a place of the unknown.

I kept going. "Back then, I was stationed in California, but we wrote to each other every week. I was able to come back and see you two more times before they shipped me off to Vietnam. Mary, when I was here that last time, I took you for a drive out to our favorite spot, which was a little ways from the city. We parked on a hill up around Stone Mountain and got out of the car. We walked over toward the lake with a little picnic basket and sat down on the grass beside an old oak tree. It was early evening and the sun was about to dip down over the horizon. That's the night I got down on one knee and proposed to you."

"What did I say?" she asked with such a serious yet nervous look on her face.

"What did you say? You said yes!"

"I did?"

"Yes, you did."

"I guess your mack wasn't too strong back then, Willie, 'cause she sho' don't remember none of that," Tina just had to say.

Some things are not even worthy of a response, so I ignored that fool neighbor of mine and went right on with what I was saying. "I was so happy! We both were, and that night we made love for the first and last time. Right there on the blanket, underneath the stars, our devotion to each other began."

"You means to tell me that I let you get me naked out there in the dirt before God in heaven and all His angels? My backside was all up and exposed and my breasts was floppin' and flappin' all about in the night air? Oh no, I know you lying now, William Alexander! I'm telling you like I done told this pimp-daddy preacher over here, I'm *not* that kind of woman!"

"Hold on!" Weldon said, standing up. "I know you didn't just call me no pimp-daddy preacher!"

"Well," Betty-Jean interjected, "I done heard some stuff about you in these few moments today. They saying that you tries to be a sugar daddy to the little girls and all. Now, Reverend, that's not how y'all supposed to be acting up in the church house, now."

"Would y'all please be quiet and let me finish! I mean every time I get to going good, somebody's got to open their mouth and get in the way!" I really wanted the three of them to just leave and go home at that point. They were working my last nerve, and I know they were giving Vickie a rash. I could tell by the way she rolled her eyes and sucked her teeth that these fools were about to get told off. There had been more than enough of that today, so before my baby jumped in, I once again resumed the discussion.

"We made love that night, but the next morning I had to leave and report to the base for duty. I got back, and within hours I was boarding a military flight to a foreign country. We wanted and tried to keep in touch, but it was impossible. About seven and a half months later, I got news about what happened to you and the kids. There was nothing I could do. We weren't married and I was thousands of miles away, fighting a stupid and senseless war. I didn't even know that you were pregnant with our Victoria. When I finally found that out, I was led to believe that she'd died inside of you. I got hurt bad out there, Mary, and it was years before I was able to come back to the states.

I came back though. I came back, looking for you every-where. Nobody knew what happened to you. Some said you had died in the crash. Some said you had survived but lost your mind and was taken away to some mental hospital up north somewhere. My whole world was gone and the worst part is, at the time, I didn't know I had a daughter out there. I never knew she survived."

Tina was looking at me with the most torn and troubled look I'd ever seen on her face. She didn't have any more jokes or jabs now. She realized how horrible this must have been. "You mean all this time you didn't even know they were alive?

Willie, how did you not know what happened to Mary and Vickie? I don't get it!"

"I didn't know anything," I said, defending myself. "And I didn't have anyone who could or would tell me any different! All I had was loss and pain. All I had was a battered body, a war wearied mind, and the love of my life was gone. So what did I do, I'm sure you're wondering. I did all I knew to do until there was nothing left to do. I drank. That's what I knew to do to get away from the pain. I gave up hope of ever finding Mary and never would have even looked for Victoria until I got this picture."

"Picture?" Weldon asked like he was interrogating me.

I pulled a picture that I carry with me all the time and everywhere I go out of my back pants pocket. I was about to show it to everyone, but he quickly grabbed it out of my hand before the others could get a good look.

"Well, where did the picture come from?" he continued. "Somebody must have known about her, about you. Somebody had to know something, even about Sis Mary, right?"

"That's just it, Rev; to this day I don't know how it all came to be. Years went by and I never heard anything until I got home one day from work and found this picture. It was in my mailbox. I came in the building like always and went to get my mail. I shuffled through what I thought was nothing but bills and advertisements. I got this envelope and almost threw it away, thinking it was junk. But I opened it, and this was inside."

"Who sent the picture?" Tina asked.

"I don't know. It just showed up from an anonymous source."

Mary could hold her peace no longer. This was tearing her apart and she was having a hard time discerning what emotion to release. She didn't know if she should cry, or yell, or be angry, or afraid. She stuttered when asking a question. "What,

what do you mean from an anonymous source? Let me see that picture, please."

Weldon gave her the picture and she examined it with more intensity than you could imagine. She put it close to her face, and then stretched her arms all the way out in front of her. She looked at the front, then turned it over and examined the back. She kept turning it three hundred sixty degrees, trying to see only God knows what. Everybody got so quiet and still. I had to break the silence.

"There was no envelope. No return address. There was nothing but her name on the back. When I looked at the little girl in the picture, I recognized those eyes. Those were Mary's eyes and I knew right away, without a shadow of a doubt that this was my daughter! Don't ask me how I knew, I just did. I got so weak that I just collapsed on the floor. I sat there for hours just clutching this picture. People came and went, looking at me like I had literally lost my mind. But I knew deep in my heart this was our child."

"But how do you know this from just looking at one picture?" Mary asked.

"Because you and I said that same night when I proposed, that when we got married, if we ever have a little girl, we would name her Victoria."

"Willie," Betty said with now even more tears in her eyes. "Why didn't you tell me I had a niece out here in the world? I mean you didn't bother to say a word to me about—"

"Betty, you were out living your life and traveling all over the country with one man after the other. You and I hadn't talked much since I came back from Vietnam. I wasn't the brother you knew. That war messed me up. All I cared about was myself and my next drink. I was done caring about anybody, but when I got this picture, I promised God I would spend the rest of my life trying to find my little girl."

"So how did you two finally meet?" Tina asked.

"Well, I went and found out what hospital Mary was taken to in Florida after the accident. I got in my car and drove down there, determined not to return until I had answers. I went to every staff member in the place and ran them out of their minds, trying to get information about what happened that night. I went so far as to even retrieve the names and phone numbers of several staff members who had retired but were still living in the area. It was hard and it took time, but I found a nurse who was able to help me. She no longer worked there but she remembered that night. She remembered when the paramedics had brought Mary in and how bad her injuries were. She was part of the team that worked on Mary all night long. It was this nurse who told me that Mary was pregnant and they had almost lost her baby during surgery. I said they *almost* lost her baby, but she survived! The nurse told me they couldn't get in touch with any family because they didn't have any information. Mary was in a coma and they needed someone to care for the child. There was a catholic church in the community that worked with the hospital in those types of matters and one of the nuns was called in to take and care for Vickie until they could find a family member. They would watch over her until her mother regained consciousness."

"So that's how I ended up in the orphanage?" Vickie cried out. "I was left there with nuns? I was just given away? But when I moved out here and found this place, I asked them what happened to my mother! I begged them to tell me the truth and what I was told was that my mother had died! You mean they lied to me?"

"No, baby, they told you what they thought to be true. Mary finally came out of that coma. She came out, but she couldn't remember anything. The nurse told me one night Mary just got up out of her bed and walked out of the hospital. I don't know how they didn't see her, but she left. They searched for days, but couldn't find her. About a week later, there was a horrible explosion in an abandoned building, where it was known that vagrants would sometimes be inside sleeping and trying to stay out of the cold. Nine victims had died and were horribly burned in that fire. They assumed that one of the casualties was Mary."

"Daddy, I don't understand how they could not know!"

"It was a different time back then and they did the best they could with what they had."

Vickie was hurting, but she also seemed appreciative that the truth was finally coming out. "I came out here looking for answers to the origins of my life," she said, "but all I found was heartache and empty answers. I left the only home I knew and ended up here, alone and angry. I ran out of money and couldn't even hold a decent job because they said I had a bad attitude and a chip on my shoulder. I had to work. I had to live. So I decided to start working in the nightclubs. I was good and the money was steady, so that's what I did—I danced. I met a lot of girls who ran away from their homes because they said their parents were too strict. Here I was wishing I had a mother or father to make me clean my room or take out the trash. I wished I had someone to tuck me in at night and teach me what silverware to use at nice restaurants. God took all of that from me; so I just did what I did. The more time I spent in there, the more I distanced myself from caring. It's just a job now. I don't even think about it."

"Young lady," Betty said to Vickie, "I am so sorry for what I said earlier. I just didn't know."

"But Vickie," Tina jumped in, "I know you're just hearing about your mother at the same time we are, but you've known about Willie for a little while now. How did you two find each other?"

Wow, in all of the emotions in the room at that time, we'd almost forgotten to deal with how I was able to share in the precinct last night what I knew to be true about Vickie and me. I felt that I needed to explain that at this time, but Vickie decided that she wanted to tell the story instead.

"How did Daddy and I meet? Well, this is very interesting. Let me see ... Oh yeah. I was working downtown one night like usual, when he came inside."

"Willie!" Betty interrupted. "You went to the strip club to see your daughter dance naked?"

"Girl, I didn't know she was my daughter, and I didn't see her naked that night anyway! Would you shut up for a minute and let her finish!"

"No, Ms. Betty, I wasn't dancing that night. I was bartending. I saw him coming through the front door, but didn't think anything about it at the time. Besides, it was clear that he'd already been drinking heavy before he walked all the way in and found a seat at the bar. I thought I wasn't paying him any attention, but for some reason I kept being drawn to him. I can't explain it but there was something warm and familiar in his eyes. It wasn't anything lustful or even an attraction in that way. Anyway, he stayed at the bar until closing and it's just by chance that we walked out of the club at the same time. Well, I walked and he stumbled. He couldn't even stand up to flag down a taxi, so I propped him up against the light pole, flagged down his ride, and helped him into the cab when it pulled up. I was just about to shut the door, but I kept hearing him mumbling something over and over again."

"Mumbling what?" Weldon asked.

"He kept saying, 'Victoria, Victoria' over and over. He kept calling my name. I looked down at my chest at first to see if I had my name badge on, but I didn't. I could hear him saying my name, but he wasn't talking to me. It's like he was asking for me, but didn't know it was me. I know this sounds crazy, but something told me to get in that cab and make sure he made it home safely. The cabbie knew me, so he helped me get Dad to his door when we pulled up to his building. When I made it home that night, I couldn't sleep at all. The next morning, I went back to the apartment, knocked on his door, and that's when we found out. The rest is history."

I listened to Vickie talk about that night and I, too, remembered it like it was yesterday. I reached over and hugged her, and tears started welling up in both of our eyes. It was so peaceful and serene for a short minute. It was peaceful until Mary pulled something out of her pocket and asked me a question.

"Did you give this to me?"

The last time my legs became this weak is when I got that picture in the mail. I couldn't believe what I was seeing! Mary had pulled a dirty brown cloth out of her pocket that was covered with lent and oil, or grease, or something. I didn't want to touch it at first, but she put it in my hand and began to unravel the material as I watched. I was nervous that it was a dead bug or worse. I didn't know what to expect. She unfolded the final part that was hiding what was inside.

"My God! Mary … Is this really … Do you know … How is this possible?" I sat there, holding this rag in the middle of my hand, and sitting so majestically atop the rag was a stunning diamond ring. "Mary, this is the ring I gave you the night I proposed! I can't believe you still have it! But how?"

"Well, I thought I found it one day. I reached into my dress pocket, and there it was. Don't you think it's pretty? It's so pretty and sparkly that I kept it for myself. I prayed and prayed that one day my prince in shining armor would come on his white horse and carry me away to Never Never Land, where we would live happily ever after. I woke up every morning, looking and waiting. I waited and I looked. I looked and I waited. I did … but you never came."

My eyes, at that moment, were full of tears and I let them fall. I hadn't cried like this in more years than I can remember. I told you I was sick of crying and I had no more tears for anyone. These tears, however, were not tears of sorrow or a broken heart. No, these were tears of joy.

"Mary, I wanted to tell you so many times who I am and who we once were to one another. I even tried a few times but you just couldn't remember. Maybe now that you know you have a daughter, that *we* have a daughter, maybe things will start coming back!"

"So, Daddy," Vicki said, "you mean all this is true? This is really my mother? Oh my God … Oh my God!"

I don't even know if I can explain to you what we were feeling here this morning. To see how three lives that were lost and potentially damaged forever were finding their way back to one another … This was epic! This was mind-blowing! This was God!

Vickie grabbed Mary around the neck and hugged and squeezed her while the tears flowed down her cheek onto her mother's neck. She was now sobbing uncontrollably and to be real, there wasn't a dry eye in this room. Mary reached around and returned the hug given to her from her only surviving child.

"You're a nice young lady," Mary said while patting her on the back. "You have such a pretty smile. Now, if God wants me to be your mama, then that's what it's going to be, okay?"

Vickie pulled back from such a deep embrace and just looked into Mary's eyes. I was, without a doubt, about to jump up in praise because not only was my family being made whole, but my Mary was coming out of her place of darkness and confusion. That's what I thought until ...

"Now come on, everybody," Mary said, pushing Vickie off of her and to the floor. "It's time to get ready for church, and I've got to lead my song this morning!" She stood up, grabbed the ring out of my hand and put it back into her dress pocket. She slung her pocketbook over her shoulder, thanked everyone for a wonderful dinner, and walked out my door, singing "Billie Jean."

We all just stood there, stunned.

TO BE CONTINUED ...

About the Author

JAMES E. CHANDLER, SR. is respected for his idiosyncratic style of writing and speaking. He is also an entrepreneur, a recording artist, choir director, songwriter, musician, and playwright. Though he is multi-talented and gifted, he prides himself on being a humble and faithful servant of God.

His message is one that focuses on developing the total person into what God has destined them to become, through the love of His only begotten Son, Jesus Christ. His purpose is to encourage every man to follow his dreams and maximize his potential.

He is the Founder, Organizer, and Senior Pastor of Marvelous Light Christian Ministries in Lithia Springs, Georgia. What began with a prayerful 250 people, devoted to spiritual growth, became a ministry, receiving in membership of more than 2000 souls.

In 1985, he and his high school sweetheart, Kelly Manning, united in holy matrimony and one year later moved to Atlanta, where he enrolled into the Religion and Philosophy program at Morehouse College. Together, they have three beautiful children, Kayla, James II, and Jonathan, and one lovely granddaughter, Lauryn.

He is truly a gift to the Body of Christ and an anointed vessel for such a time as this. On any given Sunday morning, you may hear him quoting one of his favorite sayings: "If you look hard enough, you'll see God moving in every situation."

CPSIA information can be obtained at www.ICGtesting.com
Printed in the USA
LVOW08s0113271015

459895LV00002B/2/P